Loving SIMONE

A Novel

JESSICA TILLES

Xpress Yourself Publishing

Published by:
Xpress Yourself Publishing
Upper Marlboro, Maryland
eMail: publisher@xpressyourselfpublishing.com
www.xpressyourselfpublishing.com

ISBN: 978-0-9818094-5-8

Library of Congress Control Number: 2021939577

Editing, Book Cover, and Interior Design by:
TWA Solutions & Services
TWA Solutions.com

Ordering Information:
Quantity sales. Special discounts are available on quantity purchases by corporations, associations, book clubs, and others. For details, contact publisher@xpressyourselfpublishing.com.

National and International Distribution by:
Ingram Content Group
www.ingramcontent.com

Acknowledgments

Thank you, God, for continuing to keep me in Your good graces, and blessing me every day with life and the gift of storytelling.

Thank you to those who contributed to my literary career. You have left an indelible mark and I am forever grateful.

Thank you to the school of life, its hard knocks, and its many teachers (living and dead), the sum of which has made me what I have become so far, and I am still growing.

Thank you, Bill Holmes, for being the best literary hubby a gal like me could have. I appreciate you and, most importantly, your unwavering friendship is unparalleled.

Thank you, Carolina Forest Authors Club of Myrtle Beach, South Carolina, for the constant motivation, and being a great source of inspiration and friendship.

To Mama and Daddy, thank you for everything! I am a culmination of the both of you. I miss you dearly.

To *you*...yes, *you*. The one holding this book...thank you for reading my books for the last twenty-one years! I appreciate you more than you will ever know. God speed!

OTHER TITLES BY JESSICA TILLES
(in order of release)

Anything Goes

In My Sisters' Corner

Sweet Revenge

Fatal Desire

Unfinished Business

Apple Tree

Erogenous Zone (anthology, contributor, editor)

Loving Simone (2009, 2021)

Crossing Sisters

No One Has To Know (with William Fredrick Cooper)

The Triumph of My Soul (anthology, contributor)

Loving You

ON AUDIBLE.COM

Loving You (Narrated by Kelley Hazen)

Loving Simone (Narrated by Kelley Hazen)

You never know how strong you are until being strong is the only choice you have.

— Unknown

CHAPTER 1

O nce a cheat, always a cheat.

Simone Woodson placed the handset back into its cradle. Sighing, she closed her eyes and ran her fingers along its wide base. She loved those old phones. They reminded her of her grandmother's home in Washington, DC, with the large, antique furniture covered with doilies and lace; the telephone table with the neat little phone book and the wide, old-fashioned, circular rotary phone. Unable to find one likened to her grandmother's, the push-button version was the closest she could come. She glanced at her nails.

"Who was that?"

Not bothering to look up, the even-toned deep voice scraped at her nerves like a shovel against concrete. She cringed. Gazing at her index finger, as it twirled around the long, coiled cord attached to the telephone, was easier than focusing on him, on them, on reality. What she needed was a manicure.

"Simone, who was on the phone?" His voice was tight, impatient.

She darted her eyes toward the fireplace, landing on Jackson Woodson, her husband, causing him to jump back a smidgen. Unhurried and eyeing him, she moved closer to her favorite chair positioned catty-cornered in the family room next to the open concept kitchen.

"Who do you think it was?"

"If I knew, I wouldn't have asked." Straightening his posture, Jackson was trying to cover now, changing his voice, holding a lighter ring to it. He was worried she had suspicions. Maybe she knew.

Reclining in the chair, she noted the slight change in his voice as she sized him up. "Why don't you have a seat, honey, so we can talk about it?"

"Talk about what?"

"Talk about who was on the phone."

Huffing, he stood akimbo. "I don't have time for your games, Simone."

With her eyes glued to him, marrying a more attractive man would have been much easier. Someone who did not need to overcompensate for his lack of self-confidence. Her husband was handsome, but growing up he was the nerd, the little boy the girls befriended but never dated.

"Jackson, just be honest, for once. Who were you expecting me to talk to?"

"As usual, you've got to make a big deal out of nothing." He walked past her and into the kitchen where he opened the stainless-steel, double-door refrigerator next to the counter desk.

Simone's eyes returned to her shabby fingernails. Then she stared at the Prada shoes he sported. She taught him how to dress. Pampered him. Upgraded him was the new term. Now he looked like a million bucks, even on a Saturday. He wore success like an uncomfortable vest, though wanting to make sure everyone spotted it. However, she admitted, the days of the nerd were long gone. Women were searching for a payday, and Jackson looked like walking gold. No one fell for the prettiest brother anymore after he crossed into his thirties. With his plain face trimmed in the finest eyewear, he walked with the swagger of the most arrogant of men. Of course, arrogance attracted women like flies to shit.

Simone watched the brown leather Prada tap the floor as he surveyed his eating choices. She imagined she could hear his brain calculating what he could eat without adding too many calories or disrupting the flat torso he perfected over the last two years.

She hated him. Sighing, she shifted in the chair. Not true. If she hated him, she could leave him, get up and walk out of the door. Her family would help her, they told her so. Well, her mother did. Her father only grunted, which showed a little extra effort. What she did was of no concern to him.

Truth be told, she adored Jackson. She loved him with every fiber of her being. He revealed so much about his past and his pain. They were best friends before his success. She believed if she supported him, helped him to be all the greatness she saw in him, he would love her as much. She was wrong. He grew to believe he was great and entitled. He held a different view of her as if she were lucky to be with him and to have snagged his coattail as he soared to success.

If she could only bring herself to hate him, then she could do something. Anything was better than apathy, the pathetic state she was in now.

Crossing her leg over her knee, she folded her arms across her chest. "She said you wanted her, not me." She made it a point not to pout, refusing to show any emotion. "Said you were going to divorce me and marry her."

The tapping foot stopped.

With satisfaction, Simone smiled and imagined his expression hidden from view by the refrigerator door. She wanted to laugh outright.

He cleared his throat. "Who?"

Rolling her eyes with a slight smirk, Simone pulled herself up from her comfortable chair and walked to the island counter in the middle of the kitchen. From the vegetable bowl, she grabbed an avocado and a butcher's knife. The sharpest one.

"I don't know her name. Why don't you fill in the blank?"

Simone wondered whether he was going to play it cool. The first revelation of his dirt, he begged and groveled. Then again, she screamed and yelled, cried and sobbed, yelled some more, and threw things. She was so pathetic. She remembered how he grabbed her, hugged her, and sobbed out his guilt. The woman was so persistent. He was so distracted. He made the mistake. Simone thought about the weeks and months afterward, with him catering to her every need, doing everything in his power to make her happy, buying her gifts.

That was the first time. Now, she trusted him about as far as she could throw his ass. Even when he was being faithful, her interest in him had distorted into some sad, vague, distant creature she no longer recognized or liked.

"I love you, Simone."

"Ha! You are really going for the laughs today, buddy." With swiftness, she sliced the avocado in half, slicing through the pit. She winced. She should not have used such a sharp knife. Not right now. Not when her anger was so deep, she hardly felt it.

"You know I love you. You know these females lie on me."

Females? Cringing, she never understood why men referred to women as females. For her, it ranked up there with a *bitch*. With her head lowered and eyes rolling upward, she was losing it. However, she would keep her cool. She wanted to make him sweat.

"These females? Are you listening to yourself? Should a married man even have an opportunity to use words like 'these females'? You should be out of the game, playa."

"I am—"

"But," she interjected with a hint of venom, the tensing of her jaw displaying her deep frustration. "Yet again, another *female* is calling my house, trying to figure out why I am answering *her* man's phone."

"Think about that, Simone. If I was cheating, why would I give her this number?"

"So, you could say, 'if I was cheating, why would I give her this number?'"

They stared each other down. She was close to his throat. One swift swipe and she could end it. The pain. The heartache. The betrayal. The damn phone calls.

Biting her lip to stifle an agitated grin, she shook her head in disgust. "You are a lying, cheating, backstabbing, whoring, conniving, simpleton bastard. You are a piece of shit, Jackson." Simone turned on her heels, clutching the butcher knife, praying God would give her the strength to walk away rather than slicing off his overused dick. Holding the handle too high, the sharp edge scraped against her skin. Screaming, she released the knife to fall to the hardwood floor, missing her exposed foot by mere inches.

Jackson rushed to the counter. Kindness was an emotion he only displayed when busted. "Let me see."

She swiveled around and raised her hand. "Back away from me, you—" She turned her head. Her hand hurt too much to think of another adjective.

With tight jaws, he snapped "Let me see, damn it" between clenched teeth as he grabbed her hand, pulling her close. He pulled her arm over the sink, turned on the cold water, and held her hand under the faucet to flush the wound. "Keep your hand there." Rushing to the cabinet, he reached for the first aid kit. "I didn't cheat. I let her get too close. I told her I was married, tried to get her to go away. She's been tripping."

"She's been tripping?"

Back at her side, he opened the first aid kit, retrieved the bandage, and tore at the wrapping. "Yes." He wrapped the bandage around the gash beneath her thumb. "She's been tripping. I didn't do anything. You can't blame me for dirt I didn't even do."

"Yes, I can. The world knows I'm married. They don't get surprised by that revelation after months of wining, dining, and sexing."

"I didn't wine her. I didn't dine her. I damn sure didn't sex her. I work with her. She already knows I'm married. I had to put my foot down, stop all the flirting and bullshit. She went too far."

"That means she wanted more than getting on her knees and sucking your dick, huh? She figured it was time for some carpet munching effort from your end. Isn't that right?"

Jackson flinched, mouth gaped, staring at her anger-seething eyes. He hated when she spoke vulgarly and her tongue revealed her street side. The side she patched up and covered in college.

"Simone, I didn't cheat on you. I promise. I shut her down. You know how women get. You know how vindictive they can be. She's pissed that you have a man, and she doesn't. She's pissed that I rejected her. She's trying to break up what we have because she doesn't have it."

True or not, Simone had no intention of leaving. Not over a phone call and a threat, no matter who the bitch was. She was sick of thinking about it and feeling sorry for herself.

He moved closer to her and drew her into his arms. "I'm sorry you had to hear that. I will handle it."

There was one thing Simone never doubted. When hell broke loose in his house, Jackson tightened up ship quick. She knew this woman would never again contact her. However, she was doubtful if the woman would still have her job come Monday morning. It was the power Jackson possessed and the dominion he carried.

"I will handle it, sweetheart," he whispered; his lips on her eyelid. He kissed her forehead, then her neck.

Simone shook her head. No, not this time. She needed to break through this, to move away. It was her other downfall, the secret she tried to disguise as love, but it was sex. Purely the sex. Not that Jackson was the best lover she'd ever had. Although, to the best of his knowledge, he was only her second. Early on, she decided he only needed to know about one other. However, when she felt weak, vulnerable, and scared, sex proved to be the welcoming friend to clear her mind and even the playing field. The weakness caused her pit to tingle, even though she wanted to throw up in disgust and cry at the pain of her bleeding hand. Besides, withholding sex would not deprive him of anything. That much he proved. Instead, he would cheat on her and deny her. At least she should get some sort of enjoyment out of this painful game of chess.

She let him kiss her neck, noticing how he held her arm as if her hand was a fragile figurine.

"You know I love you."

Wanting to tell him how his love felt irrelevant, she refused to open her mouth, intent on reaching a mental plateau where all of this fell away and her mind focused only on an orgasm.

"Do you know?"

She nodded, wishing he would shut up. Closing her eyes, she allowed her mind to linger on the pressure of his tongue as it feather-stroked around the base of her neck, causing hair-raising chills to cover her. He moved in a small circle around her as his tongue traced a path to the back of her neck, reaching her signature spot. *Lazy bastard*, she thought. He went right to the warm spot, knowing she would not need foreplay. A mere kiss on that spot would start her sensual flow. She stood still while he lingered over the spot, moving nearer, but holding back until the hairs on the back of her neck stood on end. She felt a tense longing for the touch, which would make her flinch and recoil as sparks coursed her spine.

"Tell me you love me," he breathed out.

Her eyes opened. Now he was going too far. How in the hell could she utter those words after being cussed out by a strange woman for being married to *her* lover? That would have been lying. It had happened before. Another desperate woman wanting to replace her. Every woman knew he was a good catch. That she could not deny.

"I love you," she lied. No, she loved him, but he sure was making it hard for her to love him right now.

Jackson wrapped his arm around her, caressing the soft spot of her belly. His lips suctioned the spot on her neck that caused her knees to weaken. She felt the wetness escape her and the tension disappear. She wanted to reach for the strength of him, feel how hard and long he was for her, but her hand felt too sore. He continued to manipulate the spot, listening to her moan. He pulled away, circling her until he faced her again.

"Do you mean it?"

Nodding, her mind now void of thoughts as she tingled with pure pleasure. He placed his finger under her chin and lifted her head until he left her no other recourse but to look into his deceitful eyes.

"Tell me again. Look me in my eyes and tell me again."

You talk too damn much, she thought. It was easier this time. She would say anything to feel him penetrate her, igniting vibrations to her core. She would say and do anything, and she knew he knew it.

She parted her lips. "I love you."

He placed her left hand on his bulging crotch. "Only for you. I only get like this for you."

I call bullshit, she thought, as she fumbled with his zipper. Simone watched him unbutton her blouse with ease and wrap his hand around the fullness of her breast. His pants fell to the floor, his erection extending through the slit in the fitted briefs he wore. With her back against the refrigerator, she never felt her feet leave the floor as her skirt bunched up around her waist. Feeling the magnitude of his girth as he eased between the cotton lining of her panties, he parted her firm surface, easing into the most intimate crevice of her. She gasped with delight, her past anger evaporating with each thrust, each deep push, bringing her closer to ecstasy and blocking out all memory of pain. Her head bumped against the refrigerator, as he gripped her hips, balancing her weight between his hands and his center mass she enjoyed so much.

He talked, questioning her with each thrust, wanting her to call out his name. She refused. Tuning him out, she only focused on the ride, receiving the release she needed. Then he shouted and jerked, almost dropping her for a terrible second, but grasping her and jerking again with continued shouting. She still pulsated. She was nowhere close to finishing. Her temple throbbed, her heart beating faster as he lowered her legs and pressed against her, resting his head on her chest.

Shit! Shit! Shit! Frustration swept through her like a sandstorm. Had he even paid attention to her, even noticed she wasn't even close to finishing, nowhere near her crescendo?

Panting, he smiled. "Damn, baby. You do that to me every time."

Nodding, Simone remained silent.

He kissed her lips, looking at her with deep, puppy dog eyes. His skin flushed as perspiration framed his face.

"Damn, Simone. Don't you see what we have? How can you doubt this?"

Nodding, she forced a fake smile. She had to finish. She had to. The intensity had its momentum, swirling into a whirlwind. She needed to feel the release of a big, swollen orgasm. The high she needed to counter today's low. For once in his life, could he not have been a selfish bastard? He almost had her there. She would have to finish on her own. What else was new?

Moving rather timidly, Jackson grabbed his pants, pulled them up around his waist, kissed her on the lips, and, holding his pants, waddled toward the front staircase.

"I'm going to go get washed up. I'm meeting the fellas for golf later." He stopped and looked at her. "Come get washed with me."

"No, you go ahead. I'm going to use the bathroom down here. I need a moment." She forced a smile. She had to finish what he started.

He nodded and walked up the stairs.

Simone waited until she heard him reach the top landing. Leaning back against the refrigerator, she slid her left hand under her blouse and caressed her breast. She was still on fire. She moaned, realizing she was unable to use both hands. The thick bandage around her right thumb did not stop the pain. Squeezing her breast, she pinched her nipple. It would horrify Jackson if he could see her. He had so many ideas about the way a wife should behave, in and out of bed. As long as she was a freak with her husband, he had no complaints. However, he often commented on tramp wives and whores who pleased themselves without their husbands, being selfish and participating in unnatural acts. Well, she was desecrating his blessed kitchen and his house with him in it.

Ignoring the throbbing pain in her hand, she held her breast with her right hand while her left hand slid below her belly button toward her sensitive knot, which felt expanded and tight. She caressed it, wanting to prolong her release, to extend the self-pleasure as long as she could. Part of her hoped Jackson would return and realize he had not been enough for her. She slid down to the floor, parting her legs wide to avoid a fast orgasm caused by her thighs touching. Her left hand stroked her bloom and her fingers danced on her swollen, inner lips.

Cupping her hand, she slid three fingers deep into the well of her love, causing her inner muscles to contract. Digging her heels into the floor, she raised her hips as she inserted her fingers in and out, the palm of her hand massaging her swollen bud.

Imagining Jackson's face, if he walked around the counter and spotted her, Simone almost laughed aloud. She continued pushing her fingers deep in her canal, listening to Jackson's footsteps upstairs, walking down the narrow hall.

He called to her from upstairs.

She imagined him leaning over the banister.

A soft "Huh?" was all she could manage. She seemed excited at the risk she was taking, the new approach to sex. Her body seemed to be responding on its own.

"I can't find any of my new briefs. The ones I just bought."

"Oh, sweet heavenly—" She inhaled. Her fingers, her hand, her touch felt better than Jackson's because she knew what pleased her and he never took the time to learn.

"What?"

"Huh?"

"My briefs. Come help me with my briefs."

She maneuvered her fingers in and out of her vagina. "Oh, yes," she whispered. "Oooh!"

"Baby, do you hear me? What are you doing?"

"Nothing."

"That hand still hurting you?"

Simone ignored him.

"Simone? Oh, I get it, you're mad again, right? I'll find them myself."

Laying down on the floor, her left hand massaged her clitoris in smooth even circles. The tremors shook deep inside of her, but she kept rubbing until she wanted to scream at the top of her lungs. Catching her breath as the sensation lingered until she exhaled, she jerked and twisted against the floor.

For several minutes, she was unable to move. When she could, she found it hard to fathom her actions. *What if Jackson had seen me, had heard me?*

Despite her anger, she could not risk letting him know her sexual hunger surpassed his by leaps and bounds, crushing his enormous ego. The true miracle was she never cheated on him rather than her staying with him. She could lose her entire life if he ever found out.

Simone dawdled to the bathroom off the kitchen. Avoiding the mirror at all costs, she used paper towels to wash and dry off, and she fixed her clothes. As she exited the bathroom, Jackson walked past her, heading for the garage.

"I hope your hand feels better, sweetheart. Take some Tylenol and lie down."

Simone nodded. She would take his advice and, at least, lay down for a while. The momentary joy she felt at deceiving him and pleasing herself behind his back faded, leaving her with a sad, lonely tug of guilt.

CHAPTER 2

"You know, I don't have much hope for you." Celeste Simmons squeezed her lemon into the tall glass of iced water and peered over her eyeglasses at her best friend, Simone.

"What are you talking about?" Simone grinned slightly, waiting for Celeste to say something sarcastic.

"I am talking about you and that man of yours."

"What about us?"

"You've lost your spunk, girlfriend. You're letting him call all the shots."

"Oh, whatever. This from Ms. Only Been With One Man." Simone lightly chuckled as she looked over the menu. She never had any free time away from her family. Dining with her best friend, Celeste, felt like a rare treat. She wanted to do it up, so she treated Celeste to her favorite restaurant, Yellow Fin, nestled on the water in Annapolis, Maryland. The stuffed salmon with crab was her favorite. "I'm ordering the key lime martini."

"Let me see!" Forgetting Simone's troubles at the mere mentioning of alcohol, Celeste snatched the menu from Simone's hands.

"So rude. You are so rude."

Celeste looked over her eyeglasses again and smiled.

Simone shook her head. "And, what are with the bifocals?"

"My new look. Thought the low glasses would look just right with my button-down and sweater. Don't you think?"

Leaning back in her chair, Simone appraised Celeste's outfit. A crisp white button-down under an off-the-shoulder sweater gave her a funky, studious look, along with the eyeglasses connected to a silver chain.

"I think they might be a little too much. You remind me of a Sunday school teacher, peering over them at me."

"Ha. Funny, funny. Enough about me, let's get back to you and Jackson."

"Look, there is nothing to get back to. He's an ass and I am too lazy to do anything about it."

Celeste shook her head and sighed. "He's not an ass. He's confused and you are not lazy. Y'all need to spunk things up."

"Celeste, you're not listening. He cheated and I can't trust him."

"Simone, sweetie, that was years ago. If you weren't going to get past it, then—"

Simone narrowed her eyes. "Then what?"

"You know what. No one wants to be miserable forever. He hasn't done any dirt since."

"So, you're a Jackson advocate now? Hell, I just had another woman playing on my phone."

"Shit, we both know that doesn't mean anything. That is the oldest move, getting you to have doubts and leave so she can take over."

"I can't believe you like Jackson all of a sudden."

Celeste pulled a chip from the basket and hovered over the table. "Ha, absolutely not." She bit delicately into the chip, spreading crumbs on the table. "A Jackson advocate? Now you know better than that. Have you forgotten?"

"No, no. I could never forget."

Simone wished she could. After the drama surrounding Jackson's first bout with cheating, she asked him to leave the house. At first, he seemed to understand she needed space. However, as the day wore on, he became resentful, saying she was not being fair, painting him to be the bad person. By the time Celeste arrived to offer moral support, he was in rare form. He and Celeste had never gotten along, but the sight of her in his house, watching him pack with full knowledge of his transgression, enraged him. When he spotted Celeste hugging his wife, he stopped packing, stared at them, and commented on how he could not believe Simone had replaced him with a "simple dike." The insult rattled Celeste to the core. Although Celeste was not gay, Simone always believed her mother was suspect, a topic Celeste protected dearly. The screaming match ensued as Celeste and Jackson swapped horrible insults, breaking Simone's heart. She was mortified and embarrassed. How could she forget?

"All right then. I am just saying…look at you. You're miserable. How long can you keep this up?"

"I'm not doing anything wrong." Simone glanced around the restaurant. Where was the server? She needed her martini.

"No, but you aren't living right either. Hair ain't done, clothes not right. This isn't like you."

"Damn, girl, stop criticizing. I am just chilling. Escaping life for a little. Okay?"

"Fine. I am sure Jackson misses the Simone that used to keep it tight."

"Well, he killed her."

"Oh, hell no. You never give a man the power to kill your inner woman, baby. Now you have really bumped your head.

While you're sitting there pouting and looking frumpy, every beautiful woman is walking past and eyeing your man."

"So?" Simone shrugged. "They can have him."

"*So*, when he looks at you to think about what he already has, how he should be faithful because of his young, beautiful wife, you're looking like this defeats the argument. Shit, if he was sitting around acting pathetic and fine men were hollering, would you keep trying to please him?"

Simone stared at her. She hadn't thought about it quite like that. Her mind was focused on how much he had hurt her, how much she gave away by settling for him. To be honest, she thought he was lucky to have her. His decision to step outside of their marriage had rocked her to her very core, shattering her idea of self and married life. Now, Celeste talked as if she needed to focus on keeping Jackson, on still being alluring and enticing. Things she had not given any thought to in months.

"Hello," Celeste called in a singsong fashion. "You're just going to sit there and look at me crazy?"

Simone shook her head. The server finally arrived, replacing the chips and taking their drink orders.

"It's just…" She sighed and rolled her eyes. "I feel like he owes me. Like he did something wrong and he should work to make it right."

"*Shit!* This is the real world, girlie. He loves you, so he's still there. But, if you don't get it together and let that past stuff go, he can always move on." Celeste popped another chip into her mouth. "Now, we both know you can't be replaced, but what does a man know? And is he going to waste time watching you moping around instead of getting out there to figure that little piece of wisdom out on his own?"

Simone stared at the basket of chips in front of her. Refusing to cry, she fought back the burning feeling behind her nose and stinging her eyes. Even now, she had to compete for Jackson, although he was the one who fucked up. She had to find a way to get past it or her entire marriage could be over. She knew it was true. He hadn't worked hard at trying to please her in months, barely glanced at her around the house. Sometimes she caught him watching her when he thought she was not looking. She knew he was sizing her up and judging her as if he had room to judge. And she had not given a damn because she figured he still should be groveling to be there. However, the truth was, she did not want to be alone. Not now. She did not want to try to pay the bills and afford to live alone. She was comfortable.

"Please, don't stress it. That's what we are going to do today. Get you a full body massage. Put some color in that hair. Trim up those bushes over your eyes. Buy a couple of new outfits. It's time for you to take care of Simone. You can never let yourself go over a man. Especially because of a man."

"Celeste, thank you for coming with me. I know you weren't feeling well." Simone eyed the bandage wrapped around Celeste's wrist. A telltale sign she had suffered another recent sickle cell attack. She always bandaged the paining limb, which struggled as the sickled red blood cells tried to twist through her veins. Celeste was a pro. When she could, she would bandage it up and keep rolling, although doing so led her to attacks, which found her managing weeks in the hospice section of the hospital. Even now, Simone shook her head at the number of times the doctors said Celeste would not make it. Yet, there she sat across from her, peering over her snazzy bifocals, spreading wisdom and spraying chip crumbs all over the table.

Celeste waved her hand in the air. "I feel well enough. And I wouldn't miss a date with my girl." She sat straight up, clapping when she spotted the server. "Our drinks are here."

Simone watched as the server lowered the small tray and placed the delicate green drinks on the table. After she left, both Simone and Celeste lifted their glasses.

"To us beautiful women," Celeste exclaimed proudly, her head back and her smile wide as the silver chain hung loosely around her neck.

Simone knew she would always remember this moment, this feeling of absolute adoration and love for her best friend.

"To us," Simone cosigned with a huge smile. The first time she had smiled in weeks. It felt damn good, too.

CHAPTER 3

Simone breezed through the front door and headed toward the kitchen. Her hair looked gorgeous. It had been a long time since she had it done. Her nails were shining. Her skin looked clear and fresh. He had almost forgotten how pretty she was, how she could light up a room. He was unsure if he should pay her a compliment or continue reading his paper. Everything he said or did seemed to irritate her. He wanted to keep the peace.

"Hi, babe." *There, that sounded simple*, he thought, hoping he could gauge her mood by her response.

She sat her bags down onto the table. "Hi there," she answered lightly, her voice did not sound sluggish and heavy, weighted down.

Lately, she looked and sounded as if she were carrying the weight of the world on her shoulders, the baggage he did not intend for her to carry, not realizing she would internalize his indiscretions. This was why he refused to leave, although he had thought about it every single day since he returned. She was not the same anymore. She did not feel like Simone, like his wife. She used to be spunky, the opposite of him. He was the church choirboy who sat at the table at parties, disappearing into the background. Simone had been the life of the party, always dancing, flirting, and laughing with everyone in sight. Jackson remembered how he used to watch her and stare at her, wondered how her skin felt and how she smelled. He could not believe she had accepted him when he first asked for a date.

Nevertheless, it was years ago. Now, he mainly harbored guilt that his actions could dampen her spirits and make her feel so hollow. What type of monster would he be if he stripped her and then left her? There was no way he would do such a thing. He had a daughter now. To up and leave his baby's mother was out of the question. He had to demonstrate to his daughter how a real man should be. At times, though, he felt trapped. Yet, he was willing to suffer through it. At least for now.

He breathed slowly, hoping he could ease through a conversation without arguing. "You went shopping?"

"Uh-huh." Simone crossed the room, opened the cabinet, and reached for a glass. He watched her apple-round bottom slightly jiggle as she moved. "Met Celeste for an early bite to eat."

At the sound of Celeste's name, Jackson's back stiffened, and uneasiness set in. The things he had said to her. No amount of apologies could make up for it. He would always remember how alone he felt, the two of them hugging and comforting each other, watching him pack up his life into small, cheap, cardboard boxes. He had never felt so angry. He could not get past the embarrassment he felt in hindsight, so he often avoided discussing her.

He swallowed thickly. "How is she?"

Simone spun around and looked at Jackson, her head tilted. He could feel her eyes but kept his glued to the "Metro" section of *The Washington Post*.

"Good. She is doing very well."

"She's still with David?"

"Yep. Her one and only."

Her one and only, he thought. He could not believe it, but then again, he knew Celeste was nobody's liar. She was fine as hell, so only being with one man had to be a choice she made. He could not imagine any man, including himself, turning her down.

Simone took a glass down from the cabinet and filled it with crushed ice and water from the refrigerator door. She brought her glass over to the table and sat down. It was rare for them to sit together and talk, especially when Jasmine was away, like today, staying with grandparents. Simone sat opposite him, sipping iced water and observing him over the glass.

He lowered the paper and smiled at her. His heart skipped a bit. *Damn, she is beautiful.*

"You look really good."

Lowering her glass, Simone smiled. "Thanks."

"I mean, damn!" He had said too much. He knew it instantly. Her smile looked plastered on, one of her eyebrows arched. *Damn it. I never know what to say. I am so sick of this eggshell shit.* Then, unexpectedly, she grinned, shaking her head slightly.

"I must have been in pretty bad shape if this is all it takes to get a 'damn' out of you."

"No, I didn't mean it like that."

They stared at each other for what felt like an eternity. Jackson wanted to touch her, kiss her face, and run his hand across the top of the cleavage pushing its way up under her blouse. He licked his lips. She never denied him sex, the one thing he knew he could always have. It was not because he was so great, but because Simone was a private freak. She loved sex, although she would never come right out and say it.

"So, are you ready for tomorrow?"

She nodded. "That's why I went out today."

Another firm function meant another boring day. Nevertheless, he had to go. Making money was dependent on landing the right accounts and the distributors of work liked to develop relationships with the money managers. He had no choice.

"Did you eat?"

"Yep. Sandwich." He pointed to the empty plate peeking out from under the newspaper.

"Well, I am going to put this stuff up."

He wondered why she sat with him, why she lingered. It was not like her. She normally stayed away from him, immersed in her work, hobbies, and being a mother. He had enjoyed those few minutes with her, though. Without her seemingly weighed down.

"Can I help?" He stood with her as she reached for her bags.

"It's all right. I've got it." Simone smiled at him.

He reached for a bag anyway, his hand accidentally landing on top of hers. Her hand felt so soft. He stepped forward, pressing his forehead against hers. Closing his eyes, he inhaled her beautiful, fresh scent as deeply as he could. They stood in silence for several minutes, him losing himself in her wonderful, feminine scent. He wanted to get lost inside of her. Moving one hand slowly around her waist, he turned his head slightly, burying his face into the side of her neck. Softly, he nibbled there. The more passion stirring within him, the deeper and slower the nibbles became, turning into gentle bites. His wife swayed against him, sighing.

"I love you," he whispered. "Do you know it?"

"Yes."

His heart was beating so fast he felt overwhelmed. She did not understand nor did she know how much anguish he felt.

Jackson tore away from her and stared into her eyes. "How can you have any idea? I adore you."

Her grin expanded into a smile. The smile he missed. Gently, he kissed the edges of her mouth, placing his finger under her chin. Taking his hand and leaving the bags behind, she led him up the stairs. Holding her from behind, his hands rested on her waist, his face buried in mounds of curly hair, Jackson relaxed and allowed himself to be lost in the sweet effervescence of his wife. He hoped his wife had finally returned.

CHAPTER 4

Simone looked over the ledge of the balcony, peering down at the many heads below. Where had Jackson gone? She hated it when he left her alone at these drab office functions. The only purpose of these boring affairs was for upper-level management to observe their associate partners and to read more into the type of employee they had hired. Everything was always a test, but Simone knew how to play the role of the perfect wifey. Still, she did not appreciate Jackson leaving her stranded with artificial people, forcing her to engage in the unnecessary, who-gives-a-damn conversations.

"There he is." The white woman sitting next to her pointed.

Simone was unaware the woman had been watching her or knew she was looking for Jackson.

"Out of the restroom, to the corner bar for drinks." The woman fished for a compact in her purse. Pausing to open it, she glanced at Simone with a knowing smile. "I hate being left alone at these things, too. Always know where mine is. Right now, he is directly below us trying to schmooze his partner. It won't work, though, he's an asshole." She laughed at her own politically incorrect statement. "Anna Stein, nice to meet you."

Simone offered her a genuine smile. She loved women who refused to be defined and not afraid of being forward. Kind of like Celeste. Simone lacked the courage to be one of those women.

"Simone Woodson. It's very nice to meet you."

"I watched yours when he walked away. Wondered whose group he is in since I haven't met him before."

"Oh, he's not a lawyer. He's in accounting and finance for the firm."

"Ahhh. So, he has a little less work to do tonight, huh?"

Simone shrugged. "It seems to me he is always working the room, anyway."

"Overachiever. I know the type well, believe me, hon. Lawyer, accountant, this room is reaming with Type A personalities. They just can't help themselves."

Simone laughed infectiously. Jackson was the most anal-retentive person she had ever met. She noticed how he seemed right at home in this crowd while she longed for her comfortable sofa and a good romance novel. She looked at Anna again, noticing she was in perfect shape, not an ounce of fat anywhere on her lean frame. Her ballroom gown was slightly inappropriate. Intent on letting her body show, per the long front and back V-shapes, which would have been a problem had she had any cleavage, but looked perfectly normal against her flat chest. She sported a stunning diamond pendant with matching diamond teardrop earrings. Her features were perfect—perfect-shaped nose, high cheekbones, pouty lips painted in stunning red—all downplayed by a blunt bob haircut for her raven red hair.

"Got to watch him, though." Anna nodded at her, tilting her head slightly. "Not just yours, all of them," she continued in a conspiratorial whisper, slightly leaning forward. "The firm purposely hires young, hot, needy women as the," she curled her index fingers into quotation marks, "support staff. One of the perks of this firm. Looks the other way when the gentlemen handle the needs with the help."

The shock of discovery hit Simone full force. "No!"

"Oh, honey, very much yes. See the blonde at the far table against the back wall? Over there." She pointed a French-manicured finger over the rail. "The one that's just off her mother's tit. Yeah, she's been my husband's assistant for the past year. I invited her to the house for a social and to let her know I am ahead of the game."

"You did? How did that work out?"

"Well, let's say this time I was able to nip it in the bud. She is more loyal to me than him, that's for sure. I know all his business, but I wasn't always so astute."

Simone sighed and leaned back in her chair. Here was this beautiful, forty-something bombshell openly admitting her raggedy-ass husband was sticking his man-business in other places, and she talked about it like strategizing and fighting for him. For the first time, Simone removed the self-pity aspect of the situation. She had gone about this all wrong.

"So, is he worth it?"

"Oh, honey. That's not the question. If that were the question, the answer would be hell no, for him or any man. But I need him. I love him. And I will be damned if I lose what I have built over the past decade to some cutie who can give deep throat." She cocked an eyebrow, adding emphasis to her statement.

Simone laughed, bringing her hand up to stifle her laughter. She could not believe Anna had said that.

"You are a bit more modest than me. More conservative." Anna laughed, shaking her head. "Sometimes, I get ahead of myself. I hope I didn't embarrass you, or myself."

"No, absolutely not." Simone lifted her wine glass and took a small sip of the dry Chardonnay. "I appreciate your honesty. Really."

"So, who is your husband's helper?"

"Actually, I don't know."

"Hmmm. That means he is uncomfortable introducing her. She is probably overaggressive. Make sure he points her out when he comes back."

"I damn sure will." Simone smiled with a nod.

"But I would bet my money on the brown bombshell sitting against the far wall. She has had her eye on you since you sat down."

Simone sat up to look around.

"Don't look yet…" Anna hesitated, glancing past Simone's head. "Okay, turn slightly."

Simone obeyed.

"See her?"

Yeah. I see her ass.

"I never saw her at one of these before," Anna admitted. "But it's just an educated guess."

Simone felt her anger rise. The girl looked like she could belong to the thick voice that had called a few days before. If it did not belong to her, the woman damn sure knew the owner of that voice.

Simone patted Anna on the hand. "I think you're right. I am going to find out right now."

"No, no, no." Anna clicked her tongue. "No scenes, no fights. Not here."

"Oh, no. Watch how I handle this."

Simone stood slowly, adjusting the deep green body con dress perfectly hugging her. She loved this dress. She and Celeste had spotted it together, and she knew she could rock it, with the help of a girdle and control top pantyhose. However, with the easy flat look achieved, Simone made her way slowly across the room, seemingly intent on finding the restroom. She made eye contact with the only other Black woman on that side of the balcony dining area and gave her a *How are you?* sister nod, the acknowledgment of one Black woman to another. Simone knew instantly the woman was unsure of how to respond. If she ignored Simone, it would give Simone reason to pause and ponder, something she did not want. After an awkward split fraction of a second, the woman smiled warmly and nodded.

Taking the nod as approval to approach, Simone walked to her. "Excuse me." Simone smiled. "Are there any restrooms on this level?"

"Oh, no." The voice sounded higher than she had anticipated. "No, you have to go down near the portraits. The restroom is on the other side."

"Thank you." Simone rolled her eyes dramatically. "I have no idea where my husband went and I hate these things. Do you work for the firm?"

"Uhm, uh, yes, I do. I think…actually, are you Mrs. Woodson?"

Bingo. Simone smiled. "Yes."

"I am Mr. Woodson's assistant. India Walker. It's very nice to finally meet you."

"India?"

"Yes."

"Oh, please call me Simone. I didn't realize Jackson had a new assistant."

India glanced around, apparently embarrassed and unsure of how to continue, not wanting to misspeak. "Uh, yes, I was assigned to him this week. His last assistant was, um, well, she decided to pursue other opportunities."

"Really?" *I bet she did. After she called me, and Jackson fired her.* Simone wondered how much information India had and exactly how loose-lipped she could become. However, she never got a chance to go any further with her questioning as she felt a pair of hands slip around her waist.

"India. I see you've met my beautiful wife, Simone," Jackson announced proudly.

Simone glanced at India, noticing she looked as if she wanted the floor to open up and swallow her.

"Yes, Mr. Woodson, she was just looking for directions to the restroom."

Why did she offer him an explanation? Simone knew then Jackson had probably threatened anybody about coming near her or speaking to her, and, certainly, were not to give her any information.

"Well, India, I am going to make my way to the ladies' room." She turned slightly from Jackson, whose touch felt disgusting to her now. "Thank you on the heads up," she said lightly, giving India a conspiratorial nod.

Jackson looked back and forth between the two. Seeing how Simone did not look upset, he grinned amicably at both women before escorting Simone to the restroom. Simone would not tell Jackson what she knew about his other assistant. She refused to burn the bridge to India so easily. As she and Jackson walked past the small cocktail table, Anna raised her glass with a classic smile. Simone grinned in return.

"So, I didn't know you had a new assistant."

"Yeah, I like India. She's knowledgeable about the subject matter and more helpful with my filing."

"Hmm." Simone felt Jackson stiffen. She leaned over and kissed his cheek. "You look handsome tonight."

She smiled as he puffed his chest out a tad bit. "You know I do. I am rocking this tux, damn it."

They both laughed and Simone shook her head as she made her way into the ladies' room.

CHAPTER 5

Simone sighed as she glanced in the mirror. She knew Jackson would want to make love tonight. Last night had been their most romantic night since he returned from his business trip.

Still, oddly enough, she had not felt satisfied. She tried to force it from her mind and concentrate on pleasing him. Normally, pleasing him, which made him call out her name or stare at her in wonder, did the trick. Last night, though, after the first time when she barely felt a sensation, she went through the motions faithfully and wondered when she could get away to satisfy herself.

She could not stand another night of unfulfilling sex. What was wrong with her? He had not changed. He used to be enough. She had felt like he was the best lover in the world and would moisten at the simple thought of him. Now, she thought about her to-do lists during sex, pondering if the credit card company received the payment before the due date.

She found herself looking at other men. Tonight, the waiter serving the wine seemed incredibly attractive. She had lowered her head slightly and devilishly grinned when he handed a glass of white wine to her. She hoped he had not noticed, but he kept checking on her every few minutes. His direct looks and sensual body language informed her she could have him in any way and at any time. That sent exciting chills throughout her. Here she stood in the bathroom, with Jackson waiting in the hallway, and she could imagine the waiter's thin lips on the edges of her labia, licking gently along the inside of her thigh. She had never been with a white man, so she had no clue how they made love. She wanted to find out, though. It would feel refreshing, probably, to make love to him in the back while Jackson strutted around like an overconfident peacock. She imagined her back against the wall, legs spread apart, lifted high in the air, bouncing up and down in unison to the waiter's thrust. She closed her eyes, took in a deep breath, and exhaled. "Have mercy," she mumbled.

Simone bit her bottom lip and shook her head. She studied her face in the mirror, hoping the lust inside of her was not pouring through. However, she suspected it was, and Jackson could smell sexual arousal a mile away. Before she met Anna, two of her husband's coworkers had stopped by her table to chat. When each came by, it was a very friendly "Hi" followed by a warm accommodating hug. Within minutes, though, she imagined the taste of their lips and the powerful stroke of their muscles. Both lingered a little too long, chuckled a little too seductively, looked a little too deeply into her eyes.

She could not pinpoint what was wrong with her. She was normally shy when first meeting men and would flirt loosely for fun, but never with a deeper motive. Now a craving seemed to overtake her, an unbelievable appetite for men and the unique pleasure they brought, and she felt like a child in a candy store. She wanted to sample it all. To hell with cavities.

Simone sighed deeply and checked her mascara. Smoothing her dress, she left the restroom and bumped into

Jackson. *Damn, can I get a second to breathe?* she thought, forcing a smile.

"I was coming in there after you."

Simone refused to respond as she glanced around the room. India had moved to the lower level, speaking intently with two white women at a table. Simone felt sure she and Jackson were the topic of discussion, although all three were tactful enough not to look in her direction. Then her heart stopped and panic rushed through her. She felt her temple throbbing as she and the waiter connected eyes. *This is crazy*, she thought, but she held onto his gaze for several seconds while she and Jackson crossed the floor, and Jackson continued to talk. She tore away from Mr. Waiter as he gave her a smile that sent her pulses racing, revealing clean white teeth. *Damn, I have to stop this*, she thought, turning her attention to Jackson.

Jackson's fingertips caressed the back of her neck. He looked seductively into her eyes as he brushed away a tendril dangling over her eye. "Are you ready to go?"

Unconsciously, her brow rose and the corner of her mouth drew into a sexy smirk. "Yes."

"You look beautiful tonight. Did I tell you?"

Simone blushed. "All this because of one manicure and facial?"

"No. No, you just look…" he paused, looking down at the floor. Then he shrugged and looked at her with adoration. "You look like you used to."

She smiled but did not answer.

He placed his hand on the small of her back and they left the large gallery.

"Where to?" she asked.

"I booked a room for us at The Willard."

"The Willard? Really?" That got Simone's interest. The Willard was one of the most elegant hotels in Washington, DC.

"Yeah, I figured, why drive home? Why not spend a night on the town and then with each other?"

She fought the urge to roll her eyes, a natural reflex she would have done two days ago. Instead, she paused and plastered a grin on her face. "You should have told me. I would have packed something."

"Don't worry. I've got you."

"What does that mean?"

Jackson grabbed her waist and pulled her close to him. His grasp was almost too tight, a shade before painful.

"You are everything to me, Simone. Do you know that?"

"Yes, honey. I know."

He kissed her warmly, his mouth covering hers so quickly and forcefully, she could barely breathe. They stood on the sidewalk, kissing like when they were dating. Simone felt lightheaded and her heart skipped a beat. A flitter of something floated across her chest. Love. Was it love? Something she hadn't felt in a long time.

Jackson pulled away and hailed a cab. Simone lowered herself into the car and Jackson scooted in next to her. After giving the driver directions, he immediately leaned his forehead against the side of Simone's head, his lips grazing her ear. He inhaled.

"I love the way you smell."

"Thank you. It's the perfume—"

"No. I love the way *you* smell. The wet, raw smell of you wanting me. I love it. I want to smell you tonight."

Simone felt a deep stirring in her cave. She imagined his perfectly shaped head nuzzled between her thighs, inhaling deeply.

"Talking like that is going to get you in trouble," she whispered.

"I hope so." He slid his hand along her calve, tickling the inside of her knee.

The taxi came to an abrupt halt, almost throwing them out of the back seat and into the front.

"Come on," Jackson whispered, throwing bills at the driver before pulling Simone from the car.

Simone worried a little. She was not fresh, not after lusting Mr. Waiter all night. She had gotten wet three different times, staring and licking her lips at him. More importantly, she cringed at the thought of Jackson seeing her strip out of the girdle. That damn dress! It did not seem so perfect now that Simone wanted to seduce Jackson.

They walked past guest check-in and to the elevators. Simone barely glanced at the lush lobby, with tall statues and flowing waterfalls. With heavy drapes and perfect antique furniture, the décor felt like Tara from *Gone with the Wind*. In the empty elevator, he pressed her against the back wall and stood a few inches from her with a devilish smirk on his face. Easing his hand inside her V-neck dress, he ran the back of his hand gently across her nipple. Bending at the knees, he placed his mouth over her hardened nipple and blew.

Simone giggled as the warm air covered her nipple. The tingling between her thighs was making her weak. She wanted him in the elevator, but the girdle. They exited on the seventeenth floor and hastily walked to Room 1707. Jackson slid the plastic card in the small panel next to the door and it opened automatically. Entering, Simone gasped as she stared around the huge, lavish suite. The wine was chilling and music playing. Jackson had ordered a fruit tray that looked perfect on display for a painting. Across the sofa lay a teddy and matching thong for her.

He walked over to the sofa. "I picked these out."

"You went shopping at Victoria's Secret?"

"No doubt. I knew exactly what I wanted to see you in. That's not all." He led her to the master bathroom suite. A drawn bath with bubbles falling over the side awaited them. "For us. I want to bathe you, then make love to you, then bathe you, and so on—"

"And so forth." Simone sighed. "Jackson, this is so sweet."

"Anything for you. Do you hear me? Anything."

Simone nodded, wondering where all this passion had come from. Guilt possibly? What type of relationship did he have with that assistant? Then, Simone realized she could have cared less. That woman had been dismissed and her husband was treating her like a queen. She took a couple of steps back.

"Jackson, let me get ready, okay?"

He nodded but did not budge.

"No." Simone laughed. "You go out there. I'll call you when I'm ready. I need to hang my dress up."

Jackson nodded as if snapped out of a trance. "Yes, of course."

He took a few steps back and Simone closed the door. After removing the dress, Simone stripped off the girdle, folded it, and wrapped it in a small towel, which she discarded in the trashcan. Then she lowered herself into the mound of suds, sighing as the warm water enveloped her.

"Jackson, baby. Come here."

CHAPTER 6

Jackson strolled into the bathroom with his shirt unbuttoned and his tie hanging loosely around his neck. The serious expression he often wore had disappeared. He seemed intent and alert, but still cool and mellow. Simone longed for him. She needed to feel him inside of her. They could have the romantic stuff after he satisfied the deep yearning inside of her. She stood before him, suds clinging to her as she stepped out of the tub.

He held her arms and pulled her in close to him. "Damn, woman. You just..." He sighed heavily.

Sliding his shirt over his shoulders, he allowed it to fall to the floor as she hastily unbuckled his belt. Hungering for her, his mouth found hers, distracting her, forcing her into another deep, long kiss, another romantic overture. Simone had to slow her hands and pace herself. The throbbing at her core had grown, pushing out all thought. She would lose control soon, would not be able to fight her search to release his manhood, mount him, and ride into ecstasy's oblivion.

The clasp finally came undone and Simone shoved her hands deep inside his pants, holding him firmly between her palms. As he muttered and groaned, Simone caressed him, teasing the head between her thumbs, as she stroked the girth of his shaft. She wanted him fully extended, which meant he had to be fully aroused. However, she was impatient. She was already wet, tremendously so, and she longed for him.

Dropping to her knees, Simone lowered his pants and kissed the tip of him. She heard him exhale loudly. She held firmly, turning her head at a slight angle before taking him into the moist, warmth of her mouth. His muttering increased; his talking filled with praise. Repeatedly, Simone tasted him as her excitement mounted. Her nipples were hard, her vagina dripping. She placed one hand between her crotch, knowing he would not notice, and gently massaged herself. Her juices and the smell of sex turned her on, increasing her sensation of love.

She could hear Jackson talking, but the words were not sticking. He was lifting her by the arms, pulling her up from her knees, and hoisting her up. Her hips rested awkwardly on the sink, as her legs wrapped tightly around his waist, locking at the ankles. While nibbling the base of his ear, she held him in her hand.

"Please, Jackson. Please. I need to feel you."

The first plunge felt so good and deep, Simone threw her head back, closing her eyes tight as she freed her mind. She could feel him pull back and plunge again slowly, allowing her to feel every part of him. She sighed, holding on to him for dear life. Pushing her legs back, bending them at the knees, each knee pressed against his chest as he plunged deeper inside her. Simone exclaimed in delight, the position allowing him to tickle her G-spot with each stroke. They enjoyed each stroke slowly, firmly, both gasping and struggling to manage the intense sensation invading their bodies. Simone lost track of time and place. Somehow, they were on the bathroom floor, her legs spread eagle and his head nestled comfortably between them. She squirmed and wiggled. She did not want this. Not right now. She wanted to feel the thrust. She inched back quickly. His head popped up, and he looked at her questioningly. Shaking her head, she crawled back to him. Reaching to hug him, she pushed him slowly back onto the tile floor and crawled on top of him.

Within seconds, she felt him again, plunging upward into the depths of her triangle. She shifted her legs, widening them, closing them, twisting sideways, then leaning over him, letting her breasts graze against his chest. His strokes became more powerful. His hand groped her full breast while his mouth covered the other nipple. Spreading her legs wider, she rocked her hips and rode up and down, stroking her swelling against his heated steel with each hip roll. He gripped her ample behind and suddenly groaned, twitched, and spasmed. She was not done.

Opening her eyes, she stared at him, his face completely satisfied, his eyes closed. She was not finished. She wanted to finish.

"Baby, that was wonderful." He rose to kiss her and suck her neck. Then he pulled her close.

Inside, she felt like crying. If she pleased herself, he would be hurt and offended. On the other hand, though, he did not seem to care she had not finished. He had not given it a second thought.

"Let's go to bed. I need to rest. We'll take a bath in a little while." He stood, and she avoided his eyes, trying to deal with the disappointment invading her mind.

"Uhm, I'm going to wash up a little now," she muttered. "I'll be in there in a second."

He smiled, softly bit her bottom lip, patted her bottom, and strolled out of the bathroom. She watched him fall across the king-sized bed before closing the door, with her head hung low. Feeling sad, Simone sat in the cold water, the suds having dissipated into a thin layer of residue. She felt the heat and passion fade away as her body protested the cool water. What could she do? It had been a lovely night; how could she complain? He had paid for this expensive suite and treated her like a princess. What more could she want? An orgasm would work.

Sighing, Simone washed quickly and dried off. She rubbed herself down with the sesame oil-scented lotion and pulled the tight negligee and thong over her thick hips. She exited the bathroom and sat on the edge of the bed. Jackson's snoring filled the room and tugged at Simone's heart. She wanted to wake him up. Crawling over him, she kissed his lips and whispered his name.

Jackson mumbled in his sleep.

"Are you ready for me? You ready to finish what you started?"

"Uh-huh," he grunted, and the snoring continued.

Simone pressed against him, but he wrapped his arms tightly around her, turning onto his side. Spooning her, he kissed her lightly, and the snoring continued. With the roll of her eyes and a deep sigh, Simone pushed away and searched for the television remote, ignoring the ringing alarm of disappointment.

CHAPTER 7

S imone shifted the phone to her other shoulder, searching the kitchen drawer for her earpiece. "Huh? I can't hear you."

Jasmine had every ringing and singing toy spread on the floor as she stumbled between each, giggling with delight every time one made a sound.

"I asked you how old you are."

"Thirty-one. No, two." Her fingers groped around inside the drawer as she spotted Jasmine with the earpiece. "Jasmine, baby, don't put that in your mouth." Simone ran over to Jasmine, prying it from her precious fingers as she screamed to the top of her lungs. "Hold on, Aunt Jade." Simone kissed and hugged Jasmine, then distracted her with the Fiesta Dora doll. "All right. Can you hear me?"

"Girl, you need help. All that confusion with only one child?"

"No, I just lost my earpiece."

"Anyway, you are peaking, that's all."

"Peaking? Please." Simone glanced at the clock. Jackson would be home soon. She checked the crockpot, glad for the warm meal brewing.

"Peaking, sweetheart. Women in their early thirties peak sexually. You have the sexual libido of a seventeen-year-old boy right now."

"Did you actually say 'libido'?" Simone released a hearty laugh. Her aunt was only four years older, and they were close.

"All right. Ha-ha, hell. Your ass is in heat and you're calling me, talking about 'What's wrong with me? I am wanting strangers.' You'd better take it seriously, sweetheart. You are probably releasing pheromones."

"So, what, I'm a puppy now releasing pheromones?"

"Don't believe me? Ask a doctor."

Simone leaned against the counter. "No, I believe you. I have to believe you. My body is on fire and Jackson is like a sprinkle of water. Not enough."

"Be careful. Don't ever talk about your man at home."

"He isn't here."

"Doesn't matter. Doesn't matter where he is. You never know when he will pop up or come in through a different door. How much do you lose if he hears you? Just don't play with it."

"Well, he isn't a damn saint."

"He doesn't have to be." They chuckled. "So, when am I going to see Jasmine?"

Simone continued talking to Jade. She heard the garage door opening and grabbed the bowls out of the cabinet. "Auntie, I'll call you back."

"Yeah, yeah. That man of yours must be home."

"I call you later, Auntie." Simone hung up as the back door opened.

Jackson's head poked through it. He looked good. An immaculate pink, blue, and silver printed tie hung flawlessly against a baby blue shirt and deep gray suit. She nibbled her bottom lip. She hoped he noticed her skirt and high heels. His expression was serious, his eyebrows furrowed. He scanned the room without as much as a nod.

"Hey, honey." Simone reached out to kiss him, but he walked past her.

"Hey." Picking up Jasmine, he planted a kiss on her forehead, put her down, and kept walking.

"I am getting dinner ready."

"I already ate." His voice traveled heavily throughout the house.

"You did?"

No answer. He had been this way for two months. After the hotel, she thought things would have gotten better. Instead, it felt worse. He went back to not looking at her, not observing her. He treated sex with her as a second thought, a late-night hump becoming a five-minute, uneventful affair. Meanwhile, she ached for the caressing touch of a man. Any man. A simple conversation with a man at work left her wet, her intimate parts throbbing with such intensity she had to go to the bathroom. It had only taken a few rubs with her palm before she exploded, stifling her moans as she gripped the disability bar in the large stall to keep from falling to the floor.

More men noticed her and flirted with her than ever before. Every smile from her seemed to get an extra kind response from the man with whom she spoke. No matter the race, men across the board were noticing her in a new way. She took extra care getting dressed in the morning, rubbing her skin with scented oils, and dressing in her sexiest underwear. Although she had no plans for an extramarital affair, she was quickly approaching the yearning point of no return. The right man on the right day would be one hell of a lucky man.

She had always been faithful to her husband, but this wasn't about cheating. She did not want another relationship nor did she need to engage in conversation. She wanted to see the penis, grab it in her hands, or rub its tip against the softness of her lips. She had images of being pressed flat against a wall naked, her nipples rubbing gently against the cold surface, with her legs spread apart. She hoped to meet a man with raw sexuality that would lick her inner thighs, fondle her butt, lift her to the tips of her toes and push her wide bottom over his instrument of love, lowering her onto his masculinity. She wanted a man who knew how to hold her waist and stroke her sweet spot from behind, biting her neck and rubbing her stomach.

The fantasies consumed her. During work, while typing case briefs, she found herself clenching her knees, enjoying the steady, mounting tension between her thighs. She could climax without touching herself, depending on the particular circumstance and her mindset. However, she would rather not behave this way, acting like an animal instead of a lady, which was why she had contacted Jade.

"Da Da." Jasmine crawled quickly behind Jackson, abandoning her new walking achievements to get to him as quickly as possible.

"Come on, sweetheart." Simone lifted Jasmine and carried her to her bedroom. "Jackson, where are you?"

The upstairs of the house was empty. Simone walked back downstairs.

"Jackson?"

"Back here."

He sat at the computer, his jacket on the back of his chair and his tie tossed over his shoulder. Jasmine whined.

"She wants you. She was hurt you walked away."

"Come here, baby girl." Jackson smiled fully as he opened his arms and drew his daughter close to him. It was more enthusiasm than she ever saw from him. Lately, he only seemed focused on his work and Jasmine.

Simone turned and headed to her bedroom. At least Jasmine had a man in her life.

CHAPTER 8

Simone nibbled on her bottom lip, enhancing the deep caves of dimples in her face. His eyes were still on her, watching through the glass window. She almost felt afraid to walk, certain she would fall flat on her face in the new heels she had finally felt bold enough to sport. Brown, pointy-toe slingbacks, and a business suit with a pink silk camisole made her the center of attention. He had seemed nice enough when she first stepped into the bank, as he came forward to assist her. She had seen him around for months— glances and smiles, holding doors and elevators. They bumped into each other in Au Bon Pain once, and her soup fell to the floor. He apologized and smoothly ordered her another, asked her name, and paid for her meal.

She had not realized he was the manager of the bank. Located on the first floor of the building where she worked, Simone had ignored this particular bank for years. However, she needed to save a little more money without having to answer for it. Just in case. She would not allow herself to consider "just in case of what." She simply ended the analysis that she needed another account, unknown to Jackson. Just in case. The bank manager looked like manna from heaven to Simone. She recognized him immediately. Her heart skipped several beats. As he spoke, she wondered how wide his tongue was and long it could extend. Would he be able to lick the entire width of her in one stroke? *Stop it!* she thought and shook it off.

"So, Simone Woodson, right? From Wilson Myers and Holt? How may I help you?"

She forced a smile. *Damn, how did he know all of that?* she thought, with a raised brow.

"Yes. I need to start a checking and savings account."

"Oh, I can help you with that."

Simone nodded and eyed his full lips, as naughty thoughts raced through her mind. *I bet you can.*

She followed him to the large office in the back of the bank. Another manager sat in a small cubicle alone. With her hair pulled back into a bun at the nape of her neck and a small neat bang, she wore a too-tight blouse. Her chocolate skin wrinkled as she rolled her eyes at Simone. For some reason, the move empowered Simone, affirming her femininity.

"Ms. Woodson, have a seat." He sat opposite her, giving her a simple smile as he searched through desk drawers. "Hold on, I don't normally do this. I don't have the forms."

Simone glanced up with a questionable look as he rushed out of the office. If he did not normally do this, then why was he helping her?

When he returned, she noticed the bulge on the left side of his zipper. In an attempt to keep her mind clear, she stared at the desk, determined to stay focused.

"How much would you like to deposit?"

"Five hundred dollars in savings and two hundred in checking." Simone removed the cash from her wallet and handed it to him. His hand purposely brushed against hers, the touch electrifying her arm. This tall, seductive-looking man was the color of wheat with a smooth bald head. Simone wondered how his superbly shaped head would feel pressed between her thighs, her hands rubbing over the smooth round surface. The navy-blue suit and cream shirt fit his tight physique perfectly.

"So, it's Mrs., huh?"

Grimacing, she nodded. She had worn her ring.

"I'm Tim. Tim Wills." He became quiet after glancing at the ring, his eyes now on the document. He gave her brief instructions and information, pointed out where she should sign, and quickly completed the transaction. They barely spoke and Simone waited quietly, feeling foolish for thinking he might want her and embarrassed at her nasty thoughts.

When they finished, he sat back in the chair, watching her fold the information into her folder.

"So, are you happily married?"

Startled at the sudden return to familiarity, she looked up. Smiling, she relaxed her shoulders and shrugged. "It's okay."

"Okay, huh?"

"Yeah."

The tension in the room grew as they stared each other down. Would he take the risk and step out of his professional role?

"Are you faithful?"

There it was. He had stepped out on a professional limb.

She nodded slowly; her eyes locked on his. "Yes. I always have been."

"Is he faithful to you?"

Simone shrugged and gave a pitiful smile. "Hell no!" was what she wanted to scream, but instead she said, "No way for me to know."

There was nothing else to be said. Silence hovered over the room like a dark cloud, and Simone watched Tim's full lips. They turned up into a sarcastic smirk. That was when Simone realized he knew how to play this game and he was playing it well.

She stood up. "Well, thank you."

Tim followed her lead and stood. Quickly approaching her from behind, he waited to walk her out. "Well, if you ever need other options, here is my card."

"Really?" Simone grinned. *This brother is too smooth. He must be a hoe*, she thought, looking at the card he extended toward her. However, she could have cared less. She did not want another man or a relationship. Therefore, an educated hoe, in charge of a bank, was not such a bad option. "Thank you."

As she reached for the card, he caressed her hand and stepped in close. Their interaction felt surreal as Simone realized they wanted the same thing. His bulge was protruding, and she had a deep yearning to fondle it. Why was it that she could not be a woman who simply acted on her urges and worry about the consequences later? Because that had never been her, and the truth was, she would be selling herself and her marriage short. Yet, she wanted to feel that bulge.

As Tim stood a step from her, her eyes were on his chest and she knew he was watching her. He leaned down and gave her a quick peck on the cheek. Intimate enough to demonstrate that he was not afraid, but distant enough to avoid him being labeled an aggressor. It did not matter to Simone. The door was closed, and she was going for it. She inched up on her toes and kissed the side of his neck. When she turned to walk away, he grabbed her arm, pulled her into

him, and kissed her passionately. Before she had any clue
what was happening, her skirt was hiked up around her waist
and she was propped up on the desk, while this stranger was
pressed up against her, his tongue exploring the insides of
her mouth.

Simone tried to collect her thoughts. She could not find
a way to remove herself and to end it. She did not want to.
She felt hot enough to explode and the pressure of his bulge
rubbing against her activated her thighs like an automatic
door.

There was a light tap at the door. He pulled back a few
inches, slowly and calmly, unfazed that being caught would
probably mean his job.

"Yes, I am with a client," he quickly responded to the
intrusion.

"We have a gentleman here who needs a large wire transfer."

"Just a few minutes. We are finishing up now."

Tim smiled at her; his lips pressed against hers. She could
feel his smile tickling her lips. Without moving back, he said,
"When you're ready for this, call me."

She nodded and smiled back. This man seemed too good
to be true. He was exactly what she needed. He moved back
slowly and held her hand. She took a second to run her hand
through her hair and straighten her skirt. When he opened
the door for her, the woman who had rolled her eyes was
standing there with an evil scowl. Simone ignored her and
walked by, making a mental note to never take or deposit
money there while that woman was around. Her eyes glazed
over as she looked at Tim. He seemed as cool as a breeze and
gave her a slight nod behind the woman's back.

As Simone stepped lightly across the long marble hallway,
she tucked Tim's number into her suit pocket. That had been

so easy. She did not want to glance back across the lobby through the huge picture window, but curiosity was getting the best of her. Did Tim do this so much that he would not even remember her once she had left? She lowered her chin slightly and turned her head in the direction of the bank. He stood, talking to the client, his eyes focused on her over his client's head. She smiled. She wanted this man and there was no reason not to indulge. There was no reason why she could not oblige the blooming woman inside of her that called for a more attentive touch than that administered by Jackson.

Simone switched into her office and slid the glass door shut. She rested her hand on the back of the chair and lowered her head. She wanted to make love to someone else. She had known it for some time but thought it was some latent desire for revenge rearing its ugly head. The realization was that it had nothing to do with Jackson. Nothing at all. She had a deep, internal longing that needed fulfilling. Jackson was not meeting her needs and her prim and proper rules of existence had faded in the face of this new, persistent hunger.

Could she do it? Simone shook her head as she sat down behind her desk. She felt the moistness between her thighs, even now, floors away from Tim, minutes away from his touch. Her hips gyrated, as if he were still within reach. "I am out of control," she mumbled. The thought frightened her, but only for a moment, as she thought of Tim's soft lips tracing a path up her back.

CHAPTER 9

S elfish. He had never put his finger on it before on what annoyed him so much about Simone. But the answer seemed so simple now. She was merely selfish. Self-important and selfish. "Always judging me, always holding my faults out to be examined," Jackson said to himself, shaking his head and leaning back into the soft leather seat of his brand-new, black-on-black M235i xDrive Gran Coupe BMW, as he cruised Interstate-95 northbound.

He had been watching her lately. This sudden change, the renewed interest in how she looked, dressed, and smelled. He was nobody's fool. She was trying to make him jealous, another way to remind him of his mistakes.

Pressing his foot against the accelerator, increasing his speed beyond the fifty-five-mile-per-hour legal limit, he nodded. He was falling for it. He would simply ignore her. "She thought she was being cute yesterday in the mall." She had packed up Jasmine and announced they were going shopping. Something about her new demeanor did not sit right with him; he wanted to test her out. He had asked if he could come as well. She stared at him coolly for a second, obviously disappointed, then shrugged.

She had to drive, too. Jackson sat in the passenger seat, tapping his hand against the dash. He would be damned if she took his daughter to some other man, or wherever she had planned to go. Jackson shook his head; he had to clear his mind. Why had he assumed she was hooking up with anybody, she had never cheated? He knew that better than he knew himself. Simone was making crazy thoughts, with no logical explanation, come into his head. He knew she was not messing around, but still, she had no problem leaving without asking him about his plans. She never seemed to care anymore, asked follow-up details, or even raised an eyebrow when he came in late. What was she doing now that she barely noticed him?

"Nothing. Just trying to hurt me," he mumbled, shaking his head.

However, at the mall, Jackson was surprised by the number of men who eyed his wife with him standing next to her. Especially while she held Jasmine. He always assumed Jasmine would keep other men at bay. Who needed a woman with extra responsibility? Nevertheless, he witnessed the opposite. Simone and Jasmine seemed to glow and men were picking up her scent like a dog to a bitch in heat.

Realistically, Simone seemed to be releasing something in the air because she caused more commotion with a ponytail, jeans, and T-shirt than he ever remembered. They didn't mind that she had a man with her. Simone did not blink an eye when a woman looked his way. She almost seemed relieved as if the woman would provide some sort of wanted distraction.

Jackson was having a full-blown conversation with himself. "Simple. She is trying to hurt me. I am not going to acknowledge it. I'll just ignore her. Ignore these simple games. The extra lingerie, the smell of sex on her fingers the first thing in the morning. Laying next to me in the middle of the night, not giving me shit, but, obviously, touching herself. Selfish."

He had spent an arm and a leg taking her to that fancy hotel the night after his work social. He sexed her into submission until they both passed out. "But when I woke up, there she was with a sour look on her face. And I refused to satisfy that childishness with an answer. So selfish. Whining and complaining because I went to sleep. Hell, I was tired. Maybe she should learn how to keep up and get hers instead of lasting forever. How is that my fault?"

The annoying ring on his cell phone blared through the car speakers. He meant to turn the phone off.

"Yeah."

"Jackson, this is India."

"What's up, India? Did the partners meet yet?"

"No, not yet. I am sorry to call you about this, but..."

There was an awkward pause and Jackson felt his stomach tighten. He had not messed with India at all. He kept his word and had been faithful to Simone's selfish ass. What could India possibly have to say?

"Nina contacted Mark Royster."

"*What?*" Jackson slammed on the brakes and swerved across the four-lane highway to the shoulder, causing traffic mayhem as the idiot tailgating him swerved into another lane of traffic, just barely missing a passing car. He wailed on his horn and cursed, but Jackson didn't hear it. "India, talk to me. What is happening?"

"Word is, she is thinking of taking a sexual discrimination action against you."

"You have got to be kidding." He let out a barking laugh, so deep and thick that it sounded painful.

"Mark is talking with John now. This might not go anywhere. It might get ugly. I don't know enough yet."

Jackson sat in his car, trying to contemplate his options. Mark Royster was the managing partner of the law firm. Nina Casey had gone way out of the chain of command by contacting him, which demonstrated she was in this for money instead of protection. John Hacker was the partner who managed the accounting group. Jackson reported to him. Jackson knew John, too, had had a few discreet relationships.

"Well, John is cool. He will know how to handle this."

"If you say so, Jackson. I just thought you should know."

"India, I appreciate this."

"Well, I appreciate that you are not treating me, as it was rumored, how you treated her."

He swallowed hard. She sounded annoyed and upset. *Women*, he thought. What had he done to her?

"India, do you believe her?"

"Jackson, come on. Listen, it's not my business."

"Then why did you give me the heads up?"

"Because you're a Black man trying to play their game. Besides, they are always forewarned, shielded, and protected. It's only fair."

He was quiet, trying to read between the lines. Traffic was too thick, so he sat on the shoulder. He needed to think.

"So, in other words, you believe her, you are mad at me, but you are doing this for the greater good."

"No. I am pissed at her. Doubly pissed at you. I am doing this for the greater good."

He smiled. That was why having India was so awesome. She saw the big picture.

"Why are you doubly pissed at me?"

"Because I had to stand there and lie to your wife, and now I have to cover for you again. And it pisses me off because

Nina is trifling. Brothers always mess with a woman like her and then wonder why their business is on the front page."

Damn. Did she have to say that? Jackson sighed deeply. Simone could not hear about this, although it was kind of her fault. He would not have fired Nina had Simone not overreacted to the phone call.

"So anyway, boss man. Come in here prepared tomorrow. Got it?"

"Got it." He sighed again. "India, I owe you one."

"Yeah, I know." Her voice sounded lighter and nicer. "We'll find a solution to that problem a little later."

Jackson felt the hairs on the nape of his neck stand, a slight pound passing through him at the seductive tug of her voice. *I must be imagining things*, he thought.

CHAPTER 10

———✵———

Tim grinned widely, his light brown eyes flashing against the night lights strung over the bar. How had she missed those beautiful eyes? Those were deal breakers for her; she had never been able to resist light eyes. "You know what I like?"

"Huh? Tell me." Simone giggled ridiculously, lowering the sour apple martini and licking her lips, enjoying the salt from the rim of the glass. She leaned forward to hear better, her mischievous smile matching his.

"Uh-huh. You know what? No more drinks for you."

Simone laughed loudly. "I'd like to see you stop me. I am free tonight. So free." She lifted her glass in a mock toast. "To freedom," she shouted, but her antics were unnoticed in the loud establishment.

She and Tim had bumped into each other at the office gathering in the lobby and had taken their private party to Stan's, a low-key, basement-level lounge and restaurant on Vermont Avenue, Northwest, in downtown Washington, DC.

"So, tell me, what do you *really* like?"

"I like to get a woman so wet; she is soaking the sheets before I enter."

Simone leaned back, eyebrows raised, mouth curved in an impressed lopsided grin. "You've *actually* accomplished this? Or it's your heart's unrealized desire?"

"You're a funny one." He smiled broadly. "I can take a woman there if she is able. The problem is most women aren't."

Simone emptied the glass, tracing the edge of it with her tongue. Stopping, she sat straight up. "I'm sorry, I got lost. Most women aren't what?"

"Aren't capable of that type of moisture."

"Whatever."

"Really."

"Really?" Simone gingerly reached her fingers into the glass. She loved the cherry waiting for her like a huge surprise. "Why not?"

He shrugged, watching her pick the cherry out of the glass and rub it slowly across her lips with her eyes closed.

Sighing, she opened her eyes and rested the cherry on her tongue. "Want some?"

"Definitely." Tim chuckled. "But I will let you have all of *that* cherry."

"Ooh, you are so nasty. I love it."

They laughed aloud.

Tim leaned into her. "So, what do you like?"

Simone shrugged. "I don't have an answer for that."

"You don't?"

"Nope."

"Can you get wet like that?"

"Definitely. Given the right ingredients, I can mix it up."

"Oh, the right ingredients." Tim took a swig of Heineken while the server delivered another martini to Simone.

"Yep. I love…you know…*it*."

"Hmm. That's good to know."

"Well, no, actually, it's not. I've found that it makes my lovers lazy." Simone had to laugh at that one. She said lovers as if she was not in a marriage in which she had been faithful. The alcohol had gotten to her. "The sight is all I need. Sometimes."

"My kind of woman."

"My kind of man."

They raised their drinks for another toast.

"So, how does this evening end for us?"

Simone giggled. "I can't do nothing for ya, man." Raising her left hand, she wiggled her ring finger. "Married."

"Yeah, I know. But what he doesn't know—"

"True." She gazed at him, leaning back in the seat, licking the rim of the glass again.

"Simone, you are driving me crazy with those glasses. Stop playing."

She laughed again, remembering how good he tasted in his office a couple of weeks ago. She tried to avoid him, deciding she did not want to be a cheating wife and could not handle the guilt. However, they kept bumping into each other and, truth be told, she did not want to avoid him. He was simply too fine.

"Stay with me tonight. You're free tonight, right?"

"Yep."

"At least let me drive you home."

She definitely could not drive. The last thing she needed was headlines of her being in an accident for driving drunk. Simone sipped the rest of her martini, watched him fling a Benjamin on the table next to the tab, and stood with him. He guided her out of the crowded lounge, his hands caressing the small of her back.

"Wait. You can't take me home. My neighbors are worse than spies."

"Well, let's just chill for a little while."

Simone nodded. She could do that. "Where to?"

They strolled down the busy street, making their way to the garage. "I can at least drive you around until you have sobered up some. You must not drink a lot."

"Not a lot."

His hand remained comfortably in the small of her back and she felt giddy. A couple of times, he allowed his hand to wander up to the back of her neck, an area too sensitive to touch. She could not hide it and moans escaped her unabashedly. When they reached the garage, he kicked the gate.

"Damn it! I forgot this garage closes early on Fridays."

"Don't worry. Where's my car?" She spun around on the sidewalk, trying to get her bearings. Tim's arms were around her waist within seconds. He pressed her against the sidewall by the ticket booth, out of public view.

"I want to make you soak the sheets," he whispered, kissing her lightly on the lips.

She grinned slyly. "You have already started leading me down that path."

His torso pressed against her; those tiger brown eyes boring deep into her. She had on a skirt. It would be so easy, right there on the street. She wanted to so badly.

"Let me see that tongue."

"No." She laughed.

"Come on. Please, just once."

Simone slowly stuck out her tongue and traced his lips with light strokes.

"I've got to have you." His voice was thick with a passion that her head tingled by the rush of blood pulsing through her veins, as he, unknowing to her, unzipped his pants.

She wished she could wrap her legs around his waist, but the fitted skirt would have to be hiked up and she could not master that position. He held her tighter. Spreading her legs slightly, she sighed as her skirt gave way to his unmistakable length, feeling it slide in and out from between her thighs as he rhythmically moved back and forth. Kissing her deeply, he stopped moving and pressed her firmly against the wall. His manhood rested between her thighs, just at the tip of her temple. She started working her hips in a teasing motion, pressing her thighs together tightly. Tim moaned in her ear and nibbled on her lobe. She tingled, she found a unique satisfying rhythm, and they sighed in unison as she gyrated against him.

"Damn, girl," he deeply moaned in her ear.

Simone smiled, forgetting she was outside against the inner wall of a parking garage only a few blocks from her place of employment. She'd forgotten she was a wife of a respected accountant at a major law firm who would, without doubt, leave her at the mere mention of indiscretion. Forgetting she was the mother of a small, baby girl who was reason enough not to do anything shameful. All of those truths were lost on Simone, the excitement of feeling this stranger long for her, hearing him call for her, observing proof of his desire for her caused an inexplicable thrill that mounted her excitement and made her unable to contain herself.

"Damn, baby, stop." Tim pulled back, opened his eyes, and stared at her.

"What's wrong?" In that instant, she felt exposed and unsure. Why had he stopped?

"I don't want to do this like this. Not out here in public. Not with you. I want to take you somewhere and make this worth it."

His wheat-colored skin seemed flushed, his eyes wide and intense. Leaning his forehead against hers, his lips brushed hers as he spoke.

She pulled him closer to her, not wanting the night air to cool her. She was so close to orgasm by simply grinding against Tim's remarkable girth, she did not want to stop and she certainly did not give a damn where they were.

"No." He stepped back again. "When you remember this, I don't want you to remember it like this." He shook his head. "Come to my place tonight."

She shook her head. She did not want to go to his place and wind up crashing into a fitful, drunken, snoring slump.

"A hotel. Let's go to a hotel then."

Simone thought about that one. If she let Tim pay for it, there would be no record, nothing to get her into trouble. Then she could get to feel what she had only rubbed against. She wanted to experience Tim.

She nodded, and he leaned down, landing his gentle lips on her neck. He reminded her of her first love in high school who had the softest lips she had ever tasted and the gentlest smile she had ever seen. She wondered about him, but only for a minute, as the pressure of Tim returned to the space between her thighs, lightly stroking against her as it pushed under her skirt once again.

"Uh, Simone?" The tight, feminine voice tore through their romantic dance like the needle sliding across a record. "Simone, what the hell?"

"Celeste?" Simone muttered, recognizing her best friend's voice.

Tim took a step back, observing Celeste's narrow frame as she approached, with one hand on her hip, her face fixed in an expression of craziness.

"What the hell are you out here doing? I've been looking for you all night."

Simone blinked several times, trying to remember what Celeste was doing there.

"You invited me," Celeste responded to Simone's blank look. "Damn, girl! You called and said meet you at the office after the social. Jackson was on travel and Mama B has Jasmine. Remember?"

Simone hung her head. "Damn."

How had she forgotten? The three stood in silence, Simone staring into the night sky, wondering how she had forgotten Celeste, while Celeste stared indignantly at Tim.

"So, who's your friend?"

"Celeste, this is Tim. Tim, Celeste." Simone didn't feel like offering any explanation. Truth be told, no explanation would be satisfactory. There would be questions on top of questions she did not want to answer.

Tim extended his hand and Celeste took it, although gingerly as if she were afraid of contracting something.

"So, did you avoid me for him?"

"What?" Simone did not understand at first. "Oh, no. I mean… I didn't avoid you. I forgot."

Tim interrupted, clearly uncomfortable. "Simone, I think I am going to head home. Will you be all right?"

"Yes. I am her best friend. I can make sure she gets home." Celeste's tone of voice bothered Simone. She thought it unnecessary to be so rude.

"Can I pay for your taxi?"

Simone held up a hand to silence Celeste. "No, I should be fine." Taking Tim by the hand, they moved a few steps from Celeste, who glared at her indignantly. "I am so sorry about this."

"No. I'm sorry. I shouldn't have done anything out here in public. That's my fault. Will you be all right?" His eyes were focused on Celeste.

Simone nodded solemnly, reality gradually leaking back into her brain. Her best friend had caught her in a momentary indiscretion.

They stood for an awkward moment, and she knew Tim was considering whether he should kiss her or give her a friendly goodbye. He settled for a kiss on her forehead before walking down the street a few blocks and hailing a cab.

"I'll call you."

"No, you won't," yelled Celeste. "She is a married woman with a baby. Did you know that? You two have nothing more to discuss."

Tim stood still and, for an awful moment, Simone thought he was about to tell Celeste off. Instead, he shook his head, looked over at Simone with a concerned glance, and continued walking and signaling for a cab.

"Celeste, stop tripping and stop—"

"Simone, what the hell is going on with you? I haven't talked to you for weeks. There is always an excuse or a reason we can't meet. Then you invite me out and I watch you make out and practically fuck in the middle of downtown DC!"

Simone sighed, not knowing where to begin. She had not talked with Celeste about her recent overwhelming longing for sexual satisfaction or told her how Jackson no longer satisfied her. She had not admitted that every man she saw lately somehow implanted themselves in her mind, a full layout with them naked and the possibilities of their love. She felt ashamed and embarrassed because she was the only woman she knew with such emotions, a deep-seated insatiable lust. Her lust had become her secret, as was Tim.

"Listen, I just didn't want to worry you. I…I think I am bored with my life."

"What does that mean?"

"It means, I guess, I am testing myself and how men respond to me."

"Well, his fine ass sure did respond to the test. Now he can move on."

"No, you don't understand." Simone began slow-walking in the direction opposite that which Tim had taken. "I want to try something else."

Celeste quickly followed on her heels. "Try something else? What the hell are you saying? You're married, Simone. Time for taste testing is over."

"Celeste, please stop being so dramatic and listen to me."

"No, you listen to me. You have a daughter. A husband providing for you, no matter how misled his ass can be. You cannot risk losing everything by kissing up strangers on the damn street."

Simone slouched. She knew this was something Celeste would not understand.

After a few minutes, Celeste quietly asked, "Were you going to sleep with him?"

Simone shrugged, her eyes focusing on the ground. "I considered it."

"Are you that unhappy with Jackson?"

The judgment had left her tone. She sounded like she was trying to understand.

"You know what? It's not even about him. I am just having this feeling. It's just this thing."

Celeste shook her head, with an exasperated sigh.

"I think I wouldn't be so curious if things with Jackson were good. But it's not about hurting him or anything like

that. I just see some men and I can't help myself. I want to...
try them."

"Simone, girl, this can't be healthy. Something is causing
this. Maybe it's Jackson and that cheating thing."

"Celeste, I can't explain it. It has nothing to do with him.
I don't want to hurt him. I don't want him to know. I don't
want to deny myself either."

"Simone, listen. If you get back out there, then you're out
there. You are susceptible to disease, to drama, to heartache.
You might get attached. Even worse, he might get attached.
Jackson will find out. He will. Everything that's done in the
dark—*everything*—will come to light. Think about that."

Simone wished she had not called Celeste, or better yet,
she had remembered before downing all those drinks and
staring into Tim's eyes. She wanted to be standing next to
him, lost in the warmth of him, not hearing Celeste's voice
scratching against the surface of her mind, working her last
nerve.

"Look, Jackson won't ever know. I can keep it separate."

"Like you did with me, huh?" Her smirk annoyed Simone.
She had had enough of the sarcasm.

"Just leave it alone, Celeste, all right? If you can't
understand it then leave it alone."

"No." Celeste stopped walking. "I won't leave it alone.
What type of woman are you that you would even consider
this? Would even act like this?"

"What?"

"You heard me. I am not friends with some slut that fucks
random men based on urges."

With her back to Celeste, Simone was appalled as her
mouth hung wide opened. "What?"

"You heard me. This is what you do, by the way. Play the victim and then do some reckless shit. When you get caught, you will be back in pity mode. Life is too short for this shit."

"How are you going to judge me? Tell me that? You have some damn nerve." Simone swung around on her heels, pointing her finger in Celeste's face. "I have never judged you. Although I did not agree with the abortion, I never discuss your *mistakes* or throw your shit in your face. This is how you act when I have an issue?" Squinting, Simone's skin turned a brownish-red. She felt hot and flushed and wanted to knock the shit out of Celeste. She did not ask for this onslaught of desire and certainly did not want all this confusion in her life. However, the anger she felt at Celeste rudely dismissing Tim and then staring down her judgmental nose at her was more than Simone could bear.

"What?" Celeste whispered. *There it is*, Celeste thought. *After all these years, it is finally out in the open. I was in college, for God's sake. I didn't want to ruin my life.*

"I love you. I swear I do but *fuck* you for treating me like this right now!" Simone stared at Celeste, feeling an odd sense of satisfaction that Celeste looked as horrified as she felt. Simone walked away, refusing to look back.

Celeste's feet felt heavy, unable to move, and Simone knew she was probably crying. Simone had mentioned the past mistake, something she and Celeste never discussed. Simone knew Celeste still had not quite forgiven herself and she was careful never to discuss it. Still, tonight, with alcohol burning through her system, her desire for Tim bubbling over only to remain unfulfilled, and then the morality sermon from Celeste, Simone felt justified. She refused to look back. Simone would not console her and she did not regret having said it. If Celeste were her friend, she would not have attacked her like that and she damn sure would not have defended Jackson.

CHAPTER 11

S imone sat in her driveway with the slow, dull aching
taking over her mind. The hangover was quickly
approaching, and she needed to get into the house
before it overtook her. Opening the car door, she tried to
make her way to the house. One foot in front of the other, it
was simple. Just one foot in front of the other. Simone could
not find her keys. Cursing, she leaned against the door and
squatted as she searched her purse for her keys. "Thank God,
Jasmine is with my mom."

She found her keys and shook them lightly as if they were
a rattle. Standing, she tried to maintain her balance, wanting
nothing more than to lay on her soft bed. Jackson was not
due back for two more days. Another sudden trip out of town.
Simone never asked or complained as she helped him pack,
relieved to be rid of him. He had been acting so cold lately
that the silence of her house was more comfortable than his
unexplained silent treatment.

Unlocking the door, Simone dragged over the threshold
and stood in the small foyer. She wanted to strip as she walked,
but there was no telling whether Jackson would come back
unannounced. She could not take the chance of leaving out
evidence of her late night. Mounting each stair, she thought
about Celeste. Had she really told Celeste, "Fuck you?" That
was a first. She should not have said that no matter what. It
did not quite make sense. She never got that angry.

She wondered what Tim was doing. She hated their night had been cut short. At the sixth step, she dug inside her purse. "Can't ever find that damned phone." It was too small. By step seven, his phone was ringing. She had memorized the number, of course.

Step eight. "He's not going to answer. It's too late, plus who wants all the drama, anyway?" How could she blame him?

Step nine. She lowered the phone, sighing heavily. Just before it clicked, she heard the deep, rumbling "Hello" fill the air.

"*Shit!*" Simone pressed *end*. She waited for a moment, wondering whether she should call back. "No. Just leave it alone. Lift your leg three more times and get to your room." Her headache was bearable for now and she just wanted to relax.

The phone vibrated in her hand. Simone grinned and laughed deliriously. He had called back.

"Hello?"

"Hi. You hung up?" He sounded curious.

"Yeah, I know. Sorry about that." Simone sat on the step, holding the phone close to her face.

"Are you all right?"

"Yeah, I am. I'm sorry about that, too. My girlfriend is not normally so rude."

"No, I get it."

They didn't speak for a moment. Simone felt comfortable sitting in silence with Tim. He did not rush her and seemed to appreciate that she did not need to fill the air with unnecessary words.

"I'm glad I went to the office thing, though," Simone whispered after the pause.

"Yeah, I'm glad you did, too. I had hoped to see you again."

"What are you doing now?"

Tim laughed and Simone joined him. No, she was not wasting any more time.

"Well, I am in my PJs, on the bed I thought we were going to share."

"Hmm. You don't seem like a PJs man. I was hoping you were going to say 'Laying in my boxers, briefs or simply in my beautiful skin.'" Yes, the alcohol was talking. Simone never said stuff like that.

"In your beautiful skin?"

"Huh? Oh, damn. Talk about a slip of the tongue. Damn."

"I would love to feel the slip of your tongue." Tim's deep voice did not quaver. He was not shy. She was new to this, but his quick responses left her speechless.

She paused, trying to still her beating heart. How could his words make her feel this way?

"Where do you want to feel it?" Her heart was beating in her ears, and she felt flushed again.

"Baby, anywhere you want to place it. I would love to taste you first, spin you off the tip of my tongue, and see where you land."

"Damn." She couldn't keep her shock in. She was an amateur playing with a pro. She heard him chuckle. "You aren't shy, huh?"

"Never that. I want to twirl my tongue in you. I want to bathe you and then lick off every drop. What do you think about that?"

The warmth was spreading through her thighs. She wanted to say something clever, too, but it simply was not in her.

"You are making me wet. That's what I think."

"I told you before, I can make you soak that sheet. Let those juices flow so I can taste your sweet nectar. Lick you and get you wet all over again so I can feel your swollen pussy all around me."

"Damn. I wish I hadn't let you leave tonight."

"Well, I'm not going to ask you to come back out, because you shouldn't be driving. It's a good thing your girl took you home." Simone did not bother to correct him. "I can't come over there for obvious reasons."

"Uhm. So, you are just going to rub it in, huh? I am stuck wanting you with no way to do it. I may lose my nerve after tonight."

"Baby, we can improvise."

"How?" Simone knew that under different circumstances she and Tim would be good friends. She loved his creativity and masculinity, but her want for him precluded a pure friendship. "I want to feel you. Hold you. Taste you. Grip you in my hands and massage you until you are ready to take me. We can't do that over the phone."

"You're still wearing that skirt? Lift it up."

Simone was quiet but did as she was told.

"Touch your pussy for me. Tell me how wet it is."

Simone lightly touched the lips between her thighs and sighed.

"How wet are you?"

"I'm just starting, baby."

"That's what I'm talking about."

She could hear him moving, imagining he was turning over.

"I am stepping out of my PJs. You felt me tonight, didn't you?"

"Yes."

"You felt how hard you had me. How much I wanted you. Do you remember how I felt?"

"Of course."

"How?"

"Hard and long. Strong. Huge."

"How did you feel?"

"I wanted to kiss it. Plant butterfly kisses all up and down you, holding your wide base in my hand. I wanted to rub it slowly while I run my breast over it."

"Shit," he groaned, encouraging her.

"I wanted to rub my pussy with my other hand, make me wet enough to slide slowly on top of it." She heard him sigh.

"Are you rubbing your pussy now?"

"Yes."

"How wet are you now?"

"I am soaking. Damn, I want to fuck you!" she blurted, quickly covering her mouth. Did that come from her?

"Ow, I love it. Now, tell me how you really feel, sweet thang."

"I want to sit in your lap backward." The more she talked, the braver she felt. The stronger he responded, the more she wanted to seduce him. Could she take him over the top with her words?

"Backward?"

"So, I can feel every inch of you better. I want to slowly lower myself onto you with my legs spread wide."

"Tell me more, baby."

"I will move your hand, put your fingers on my clitoris, and your other hand on my breast. You wouldn't have to move nor do anything, baby. I will ride you until I milked you for every last drop."

"Oh shit, baby, I believe you could."

Simone listened to him panting, her hand stroking between her thighs, her breathing becoming ragged. Talking to him was bringing her closer to orgasm than she had ever come with Jackson.

Simone thought she would feel stupid doing this. She read about phone sex, heard people talk about it, and saw sitcom spoofs about it. Somehow, she imagined him with her, and the idea of her engaging in something so wild excited her more. She listened to his directions, moaned and purred as she followed his lead, which led to multiple orgasms on the mahogany steps of her and Jackson's home.

CHAPTER 12

The next morning, guilt and a pounding headache consumed Simone. What in the hell had she done last night? She had engaged in phone sex with Tim. Was she crazy? She ached from the multiple orgasms Tim talked her into having. Once she thought they were finished, he would coach her again, teaching her how to talk him into excitement and orgasm. Talking and listening to his sighs and moans gave her repeated stimulation, leading her to another peak and another orgasm.

She felt guilty for engaging in sex of any type with a pseudo stranger. The guilt seemed to be more of a disappointment in her failure to be an upright wife. She took pride in her idea of a good woman, a good wife, a moral woman. How could a moral woman justify writhing and shaking and moaning and groaning on the stairs of her and her husband's house? She passed out finally, awaking to find herself naked on the stairs with her clothes thrown all over the place. Picking up her clothing and the phone, she rushed upstairs, showered, slipped into her nightgown, and climbed into bed.

Now she lay on her back, wondering what happened to her life and the simple good woman she used to be. As she ignored the throbbing desire brought on by Tim, images of Celeste crept into her mind. She should not have attempted to explain herself to Celeste. She knew better. She should have allowed Celeste to think she was drunk and made a mistake with a coworker. Although Celeste lived life fully, she no longer took chances with the "major sins," as she had put it. The violation of the Ten Commandments was a major sin to Celeste. How had Simone thought she would make her understand her desire to commit adultery? Her harsh words rushed back to her, and she smacked her forehead. She couldn't believe she had said those things. She never threw peoples' dirt into their faces. Well, except for Jackson, of course. "Fuck you," was what she said to her best friend. Yes, she was inebriated, but she was also hurt that her best friend would be so judgmental toward her. She regretted saying those words to Celeste, but not the meaning behind it.

Celeste faced death too many times to play with it. She lived fun but clean, and Simone understood it. Why had she pressed the issue, though? Sickle cell was a daily reminder of Celeste's limitations and she always had a limb bandaged, trying to ignore or push through the pain. Simone remembered sitting next to Celeste in the hospital, certain her end was near. She was convinced Celeste could not make it out of the hospice ward. To her surprise, Celeste rose like some biblical character, well recovered and in high spirits.

Yet, she said, "Fuck you," to her best friend, and throwing her biggest mistake in her face. Simone slammed her head back into the pillow. She had to call her. No, she would have to do better than that. She would have to go to her. Tomorrow. She would let Celeste cool down and talk to her tomorrow.

Simone had to get a grip on her life. That was all there was to it. She couldn't keep this up. She had to cut off Tim and all her outside lusting. She couldn't be this person; so different from who she thought she was. First thing tomorrow, she would go to church. Then Celeste's. Then, she was going to cook dinner for her husband. She had to make things right.

CHAPTER 13

W hen Jackson arrived home, it was spotless. Fabuloso cleaner permeated the air.

"Hi, sweetheart." Simone swooped into the foyer, holding Jasmine on her hip. "How was your trip?"

Jackson felt his heart stop. Was she leaving him? Why else would she be so attentive? She looked great in a striped T-shirt and khakis with Jasmine gurgling happily and propped on her hip. He knew this Simone before he cheated on her. The confident woman who radiated love. He noticed the radiation and vibrancy were back, but not focused on him. Now that she stood casually in front of him, he waited for her to drop the bomb.

"It was okay." Jackson shrugged, trying to remain steady. He was not going to be blindsided.

"Well, I guess I'll start dinner. I was trying to wait for you before I warmed up the Cornish hens. I cooked them earlier, right after church."

Church, huh? She cleaned, went to church, and readjusted herself, he thought. She did not seem like she was putting him out, so why the sudden change in attitude? He squinted, watching her as she talked and moved quickly around, placing Jasmine in his arms. When he messed up, he would immediately pay attention to Simone, trying to make up for him being unfaithful. He remembered how the guilt tore at him, following him like a third person in the room whenever he was near Simone. He remembered how he bought her gifts and tried to be helpful.

What had she done? He knew it. He could tell. Not that he was paying attention, she never looked right at him and kept looking slightly over his shoulder. Jackson stared at his wife's back and hips. Nothing seemed different, except she was talking to him instead of sulking or ignoring him. He carried Jasmine into the kitchen and noticed the small piles of food: celery and carrots on one cutting block, and onions and peppers on another. She had decided to cook a massive amount of food. Something she did whenever her mind was full and she needed to sort things through. He had not seen a meal this large in years. The last time she prepared a huge meal, she was deciding whether she should stay with Jackson or leave him because of his infidelity. He remembered it so clearly because she threw most of the food out in the trash so he would not have the benefit of eating it and enjoying the results of the stress he caused her. Simone was layered like that, making her different from any other woman he had ever met.

Simone wouldn't dare cheat. She couldn't have. She doesn't have the nerve, so he thought. It would make her a hypocrite. She would never cheat; it would take her off the high ground position she wielded over him. He answered her questions with short answers, watching her move about the kitchen and humming to the gospel music wafting through the room. *Gospel music?* he thought. He had not heard that in a while.

Jasmine gurgled, cried out, and cooed. Simone stared at her in concern.

"She's gassy. My little sweet pea is having a rough day, huh? Isn't that right, sweetheart?" Simone leaned over and kissed Jasmine's nose while handing her a small baby spoon to gum.

Jackson hated it when she referred to Jasmine as "her baby." He already felt disconnected, and it reminded him that no matter what happened, Simone would always have Jasmine and he would be the odd man out.

He sat at the table. "So, what did you do over the past couple of days?"

"Nothing. Work. There was an after-work get-together on Friday. Celeste met me for that." Simone shrugged.

Jackson attempted to look casual, but he was recording her every word in the depths of his heart. He knew how cheating people covered, giving just enough information about the questionable event, so in case it was mentioned, they would casually refer to it in innocence. Simone never gave him that much information because she never disclosed too much about her and Celeste's outings.

"What type of after—"

"Baby, hold on." Simone slammed her knife down onto the mounting pile of celery. "I made homemade cornbread, and the Jiffy's stuff you like, but I tried a new buttermilk biscuit recipe, too. I can't figure out which one is supposed to be following the timer and I don't want to burn them." Simone ran full speed to the oven, checking through the door and glancing at the timer.

Jackson stood up and approached her. She was running laps around that place. Three different types of bread? For two people? She had done something. It was obvious now. He placed Jasmine in the portable playpen, approached Simone from behind, and placed his hands on her hips as she leaned over, staring into the lower oven. She jumped. She hadn't even noticed he had walked to her.

Standing, she tried to take off again. "I have to get the celery a little finer. I want to use it in the oyster dressing I'm making."

"I missed you. Just relax a moment." Jackson leaned into her, his lips resting along the back of her ear. "I missed you."

"Uh, I missed you, too."

He turned her around to face him. "We are good, right?"

"Yeah." She still wasn't looking in his eyes. He watched her eyes wander around the kitchen, bouncing from the top of his head, to Jasmine to the kitchen island. "Of course, that's why I am cooking."

"Simone. Look at me." He watched the effort she used to look into his eyes. "Are we good?"

Simone sighed. "Yes. Why do you keep asking me?"

"Give me a kiss, baby." He leaned in to touch her soft lips, only to find them closed.

She made a puckering sound against his lips and, with one swift movement, freed herself from his grasp.

Jackson felt intrigued. He had to know what happened while he was away. Had Simone crossed the line? He would kill a man who tried to help himself to his wife. Jackson felt a wave of deep irrational anger floating through him. She better not have cheated. She better not have stepped out. It was one thing that he did it, but the mother of his first-born child. *Hell no!*

He planned to come home to tell her about the lawsuit. Nina was moving forward and, for right now, the firm was supporting him. However, some things had come up that he needed to make sure Simone heard from his mouth instead of someone else's, but all his faults were removed from his mind as he watched Simone closely, wondering what man had gotten next to his wife.

Squinting, he decided to wait a little while. Maybe he had it wrong. If he couldn't shake the feeling, then it would be time to call on his investigator. He had used her before to make some issues go away. He called her recently to handle his latest nightmare. For now, he would simply wait.

CHAPTER 14

S imone felt panicked. She needed to talk with Celeste and make things right. The more time passed the worse she felt. Celeste hadn't returned her phone calls or responded to her text messages or emails. They argued before, but Simone never crossed such a sensitive line. She never mentioned the abortion, the decision Celeste made when they were in college. She knew the possibility of having a baby could result in her losing her life. They discussed it for days. Why suffer the shame and embarrassment of an unexpected pregnancy and the possibility of devastating her relationship with her boyfriend by sharing the news with him? They handled it and never spoke of it again.

Simone could tell Celeste resented her decision. She would make little comments about selfishly saving her own life for the sake of another. She had rested her hand on Simone's pregnant belly, fighting to keep her emotions under control. She stared at newborn Jasmine with tears, but they never spoke about it.

Then, in one drunken stupor, lusting over a strange man, Simone opened that can of worms. The thought of it made her cringe in embarrassment. She felt determined to make things right.

Lifting Jasmine into her baby seat, Simone stared into the eyes of her beautiful daughter. The guilt weighing on her was suffocating. How had she risked everything—her life and her friendship—to satisfy lust's beckoning? What was she thinking? In the last few weeks, Simone felt she was operating out of control, spinning on lust's unstable axis. In the meantime, she failed to spend additional time with her baby, neglected her husband, and alienated her friendship. She kissed Jasmine on the forehead and stared in wonder as her precious daughter giggled and cooed.

Lord, what had she done? Simone attended church three times in the last two weeks: two Sunday worship services and one Bible study. She needed a word, some forgiveness. Deeper than that, she needed an explanation, some sort of answer. She was desperately searching for something, but what, she had not a clue. Some internal void of her felt so empty, and the look of a man with the hint of suggestion in his eyes seemed to fill that void. There was an excitement, a different sort of power in the attraction of a man, and it thrilled her. However, she had to shut it down. She could not acknowledge it; it was not aligning with her character and beliefs.

Simone drove slowly into Celeste's quiet neighborhood, surveying the neatly trimmed houses. This section of the city had always felt like a tranquil section of DC, yet it was mere minutes from the politics and chaos of downtown. The property values had increased ten-fold and Celeste and her husband went from struggling homeowners to equity millionaires overnight. Simone still found the sudden change amazing. She parked the Lexus NX in front of Celeste's brick home. Exiting the SUV, she pushed the side mirror against the truck, walked around to the curb, opened the rear passenger door, and unbuckled Jasmine from the car seat. Celeste was going to speak with her, acknowledge her and hear her out, even if she wanted to remain upset. Simone could not bear life without her best friend.

Tossing the baby bag over her shoulder, she scooped a sleeping Jasmine into her arms. She grabbed the bunch of daffodils she purchased for Celeste. Barely able to extend a free finger, Simone awkwardly pressed the car's door handle. She listened to the comforting sound of doors locking and the chirping of the car alarm before heading for the front door.

It was never easy getting onto Celeste's property with a baby and all that stuff. Sighing, she tried to maneuver through the latched fence without disrupting Jasmine, dropping the bag or the flowers. Balancing Jasmine on her left hip, she used that hand to get through the fence. After climbing ten cobblestone steps, Simone dropped the bag on the stoop, shifted Jasmine to her other hip, readjusted the flowers, and pressed the doorbell.

She hoped Celeste was home. The house seemed dreary and dark for a Saturday afternoon.

"I'm coming." The baritone voice echoed throughout the house.

David Simmons, Celeste's husband, opened the door with a wide grin as his eyes rested on Jasmine, but Simone could tell something was very wrong. His calming smile did not match the dark circles under his eyes and the tight, pained expression on his face. He looked tired.

"What's wrong?"

He looked at her, then down at the hardwood floor of the foyer. He sighed. "I tried to call you."

"When?"

"A few days ago. The attack started last Sunday morning, I think. She couldn't get out of bed, but you know how she is. I couldn't get her to the hospital until Thursday."

"How bad?"

"Bad. If I didn't hear from you today, I was going to come by."

"Don't worry about me. I understand. I didn't get your messages. I'm so sorry."

He took a step back inside the foyer. "I just got back. I'm going to wash up, take a quick nap, and then head back up. Come in for a minute."

"No." Simone shook her head, her thoughts overwhelming her. She was blaming herself. "I'm going to the hospital."

"Naw, you don't want to take the baby up there. Celeste would have a fit if you brought her around all those sick folks. They have her in—" he stopped short, clearing his throat. "She's on the eighth floor."

It took everything Simone had to keep from screaming out and crying, and falling on her knees, begging God. Was this her punishment? To lose her friend after saying horrible things to her. To have caused her body to attack her. The eighth floor. That was where they put her when the staff thought the end was near. Simone's heart pounded against her chest, her blood racing. She had to get there.

Simone picked up the bag and, juggling Jasmine on one hip, rushed down each cobblestone step toward her vehicle. Her mind raced; she had to take Jasmine home and get to that hospital.

"Simone." David's voice seemed so distant and faded. "Simone, slow down. It will be all right."

Simone turned around to see him right behind her. She was shaking and crying while Jasmine patted a soft gentle hand against her wet face.

David draped his arm around her. "Don't drive while

you're this upset. You've got to calm down. She'll be all right. She always is."

Simone didn't know what she had done, how she was the cause of his wife becoming so distraught that her blood had sickled in her veins and attacked her from the inside out. Guilt enveloped her to the point of suffocation. *Why is God punishing me like this?* Her transgressions would cost the life of her friend.

Nodding, Simone loaded Jasmine in the car seat and ran around to the driver's side. She had to drop Jasmine off at her parents' and get to the hospital before it was too late.

"Girl, you are so dramatic." Celeste chuckled at Simone, her eyes bloodshot and hair flying all over the place.

Simone had to admit that she probably looked like a madwoman. She forgot to roll up the windows while she was driving. When she reached the eighth floor, her stomach plummeted, sickened by the sight of dying people, room after room, and the smell... How was someone supposed to heal surrounded by death? The nurse seemed uninterested in Simone's panic as she took her time talking on the phone and updating the wall chart before pointing Simone to Celeste's room. Simone wanted so desperately to cuss her out, but she could not risk offending someone in charge of Celeste's care. Approaching Celeste's room, she stood in the door, crying, panting from racing through the hospital, only to see Celeste watching television. Tubes were everywhere, and she looked awful, but not dying awful. Not *giving-up-hope* awful, just *in-severe-pain-hasn't-had-her-hair-done-ashen-skin* pain.

"Celeste, I'm so sorry, girl."

"Sorry for what?" Celeste spoke in a weak, tremulous whisper, clearly exhausted. Her actions were slower, smiling and laughing caused her severe pain, but true to form, she did it anyway. "I don't even know what you're talking about."

"Our argument! Celeste, I'm so sorry."

"Argument?" Celeste closed her eyes in thought. "Thirsty. Can you—"

"Yeah, yeah." Simone rushed to the tray, lifted the Styrofoam cup, and placed the straw against Celeste's dry, chapped lips. She waited while Celeste slurped. Her arms seemed to be causing the most pain.

"Are you talking about being drunk?"

"Of course."

"Girl, please. I didn't pay you no attention."

"I know I hurt you."

"For a second, but I've hurt you before, too. You were drunk, and I had just torn you away from a gorgeous man." Celeste shrugged and then winced. "I hadn't been doing that well before that."

"Damn, girl. I thought…how would I have—"

Celeste tried to smile again, as the pain caused her deep brown eyes to water. She weakly chuckled at Simone, who finally smiled in return.

Simone dropped in the vinyl-covered chair and sighed, while tears flowed freely down her face. "You just don't know."

"Girl, I get it. You know it's not like that with us."

Simone nodded.

"Plus, I wasn't really listening. I was judging. So, tell me, what's up?"

Smiling, Simone bent her head and studied her fingernails. There was no way she was going into details over her heart's newfound lust. How could she explain to her friend that she felt like she had unzipped an old shell, releasing the new sensual her? How it had started with a simple visit to a day spa, a new haircut, and new makeup. A few quiet admirations from the deep eyes of some handsome and available men awakened her curiosity, luring her into the luscious world of flirting and playing with fire. What could she say that wouldn't make her seem like a bad mother and a treacherous wife? It was too much to ask of any friend, least of all a friend who internalized pain and could pay the greatest price for it. No, her dirt would remain with her, packed around her until she could dust it off and move forward.

"Nothing. The alcohol and a little loneliness got to me. That's all."

Celeste was still really too weak to analyze Simone, to note the downturn of her lips and the pain around her eyes as she fought the desperate need to vocalize the dam of confusion in her spirit.

"Well, I love you anyway."

"I love you, too, sister girl. You know that." Simone raised the cup of ice water and shook it slightly. "More."

"Yep."

CHAPTER 15

David walked quietly into the room two hours later. Simone was curled into a ball in the vinyl-covered lounging chair, with her eyes closed. Celeste was fast asleep, but her face seemed peaceful. He sighed and stood at the foot of the bed. It looked as though some tubes had been removed. She would live. Again. He rubbed his hand over his head and fought the urge to cry. What had he been thinking, falling in love with a woman who had no chance of living past thirty? Well, she had a chance, but she was already past her life expectancy. Why hadn't he considered that before opening his heart? A lifetime of pain, of loving a woman he knew would die, of restraining from having a child with her because it could kill her or the child could inherit the deadly disease. It simply was not fair.

He adored her. Remembering how, in his darkest hour, when he was at his lowest point of battling alcohol addiction, her love captured him so completely he decided to take what he could, anyway she offered it. They lived so carefully, but sometimes it was not enough. Celeste constantly wanted to be on the go and to lead a normal life, and he was so angry with her. So angry she didn't love him the way he loved her. If she did, she would slow down and lower her risk of attack so she could have more time with him. Socializing should not be more important than having her husband. Should it?

Shaking his head, David coughed loudly. He wasn't going to do this. He was thankful and glad she already had color in her skin, no longer appearing ashen and gray. The fluids were working, and she was sitting up a little, her pillows propped up. For that, he was thankful. How could he waste time being upset with her when time was the one thing they were not promised?

He blinked at Simone and wondered how much she knew about the man she married. David never liked Jackson and didn't even pretend with forced double dates or gatherings. He couldn't respect a man like that, who was brought up by his wife, then used his newfound influence to walk over others. He lacked morals. He wondered how many women Simone had caught him with. He knew Jackson had been caught. Celeste shared some of the details in a moment of anguish.

As David looked at Simone, she stirred, opening her eyes. "David."

"Hey, Simone. How is she?"

"Better. Much better."

"Must've been you."

"No. She was looking like this when I got here."

Gnawing the inside of his mouth, he nodded. He hated the eighth floor. He wanted to move Celeste to another space, or better yet, take her home, but that was impossible. Simone watched him closely. He wondered what she was thinking as she allowed her eyes to rest on him. She seemed to be observing him, studying him.

"You're a good man."

He stared at her, surprised to hear the compliment. She sounded genuine and sincere. "Thank you."

"You're welcome."

Simone stood up like an old woman and stretched her arm out before her. "I've got a cramp in my shoulder."

"You're lucky you didn't slide right off that vinyl."

They both laughed softly, not wanting to disturb Celeste.

"I'm going to head out. I was just waiting for you so she wouldn't be alone. And I—" She looked at Celeste and smiled. "I just wanted to tell you that I am glad Celeste has you." Simone seemed uncomfortable and at a loss for words.

David stared at her for a moment, surprise shining from his watery eyes. "I appreciate that."

Simone leaned over and kissed Celeste lightly on the forehead, hoping the touch wouldn't cause her any pain. Then she gathered her purse and left.

CHAPTER 16

Observing David as he watched his wife provided a rare moment of clarity. Now she knew. She completely understood why she was searching and looking for love in the guise of lust. Jackson did not love her anymore. She had not known it until that moment when David stared lovingly at his wife. The same look Jackson used to give her when she was his everything. When he felt lucky to have her. When their relationship felt pure, not orchestrated around land mines and pitfalls. That was what she wanted, a temporary fulfillment for a gaping emptiness.

She was not going crazy. She was not a whore. She was not loveless or incapable of loving. She was a woman. A sensuous, sexy, bountiful creature, yearning the touch of a man. There was nothing wrong with that. There was nothing wrong with needing, wanting, and enjoying being wanted. The error was when that need had to be fulfilled outside of the home. She refused to mimic her mother and shut down, turning off her sensuous self. Nor would she be like so many wives, tiptoeing around life to protect their images.

Feeling her invisible bubble shatter, she reached through and reclaimed herself. David was the hammer to break against that glass. No wonder Celeste was unable to understand. She never knew this feeling. She should not have to. No woman should. Although Jackson crawled on top of her and participated in the acts, she no longer had him. His inner essence no longer yearned for her. Now she knew.

Simone pulled into the driveway and sat in the car, watching the sprinkler spray across the lawn. Could she leave him? Did she have enough nerve?

Simone could not face the answer. She did not want to think about how complicated life would be, trying to live on her own with Jasmine. Jasmine. If she left, she would have to fight him for Jasmine. There was no way Jackson would agree to weekends and holidays. No, it would be a lifelong battle and she did not have the resources he did. Besides, how could she leave someone based on looking at David's face? What would she say? What explanation would she give for staying after he cheated and leaving now?

No, she did not have to answer such questions right now. Why should she? The house was as much hers as his. She had developed her life there. Why should her world have to split apart because Jackson turned into less than the man she initially saw in him? She needed to take time to clear her head.

The large door loomed in front of her. She stared at the black door, the gaping black hole in the sea of life. She would walk through it, as she did every day, but that day was different. She found herself and her answer. The change in her was all right because it proved she was alive, could feel and in need, and deserving of love.

CHAPTER 17

J ackson sighed when Simone walked through the door. Immediately, he sensed something was different. He stood erect, holding Jasmine in one hand and a bottle of milk in the other.

"What happened? Celeste isn't—"

"Huh?" Simone stared at him holding their daughter. For a moment, she'd forgotten she called him on the way to the hospital, asking him to retrieve Jasmine from her parents' home on his way home from work.

"Celeste, is she still—"

"Oh, yeah." Dropping her purse on the bench in the foyer, she approached him and reached for Jasmine. "She's much better. She'll make it."

"Good." Jackson felt slightly helpless when his baby was removed from his arms. Why couldn't he hold her when she was in the room? Why did she feel the need to take the child from him whenever she was around? "David? He's holding up?"

Simone stared at him for a second, some emotion he could not read. "Yeah. He seemed better. Worried."

"I can't imagine it."

Simone stared a few seconds longer and then kissed Jasmine before walking out of the room.

Jackson could not figure out what was going on with her. Why did she keep staring at him as if she were judging him?

She never returned from the hospital so cold and removed without crying or expressing relief for her friend.

I bet she wasn't at the hospital at all. I'll be damned if my wife is going to creep in my face.

He picked up the small toys and jungle gym sprawled across the carpeted floor. Had she had the nerve to lie on Celeste to sneak away and have an affair?

There was an easy solution to this. Jackson held his tongue and watched her closely. The sudden changes in mood and the unexpected emergencies, Jackson would be damned if he let her embarrass him. He flipped open his cell phone and dialed 411.

Following the prompts, Jackson requested the city and state, and the hospital. Information patched him through directly, dialing the hospital.

"Guest services."

"Yes, I am trying to find a patient to send flowers."

"Please hold."

Jackson listened to the music with one ear, trying to listen out for Simone and Jasmine with the other.

"Patient directory, how may I help you?" The woman's voice was throaty. Jackson wondered what she looked like.

"Yes, is Celeste Valsey a patient?"

"Valsey. How do you spell it?"

Jackson spelled the name quietly, hoping Simone could not hear him.

"No sir. We don't have a Celeste Valsey." Jackson felt his heart drop. His instinct was right. She was cheating. He stumbled backward into the wall.

"I'm sorry, sir, we do have a Celeste. They spelled her last name incorrectly. Not a common name, is it?"

Jackson could not quite find his voice. His heart was pounding loudly in his ear and he could feel his blood pressure blasting off into orbit. He wanted to reach through the phone and strangle the throaty sounding woman.

"Sir? Are you there?"

"Yes."

"Celeste Valsey, with an *ey*, not an *i*." I am updating it now. But anyway, Ms. Valsey is in Room 812."

"Thank you." Jackson closed the phone and shoved it into his pant pocket. He felt like a damn fool. The back of his neck burned and his head ached, as thoughts swarmed inside his head. *What was I thinking? I am on some old paranoid guilt shit. I have to tell her about this mess with my job. I have to come clean before I go crazy.* How could he think Simone, his wife, would cheat on him? He shook his head at the thought. *She will never do that. She will never be that person. She is an ideal wife, a clean woman.* She never denied him sex. She was what a wife should be.

With other women, he could get his freak on. He could flip them upside down, spread their legs east and west, and take them from behind. He could teabag them, dipping his balls in and out of their mouths, or hold their heads as he pounded his magic stick against the back of their throats. He could stick his tongue into their well of womanhood, lick and suck until the honey was dry. There was no obligation, no after requirements. He had his wife. He had his family. He made sure he had clean sex with his wife, making love to her in a way appropriate for a wife and a mother.

Just as he insisted, they only played jazz in their house and, because she was his wife, she should not curse. It was what made her different from all the others. Now, his self-inflicted nonsense was invading their home and altering his sense of comfort. Calling in behind Simone and checking up on her whereabouts. He had to end it.

After straightening up the room, he listened to his wife singing Jasmine to sleep. Peeking into his daughter's room, he watched her rocking in the nursery rocker. She noticed the light from the hallway and turned slightly to face him. She seemed disappointed to see him. However, Jackson waved it off. Who else had she expected to see? He smiled and motioned for her to come into the hall. After a few minutes, she laid Jasmine in the crib and stood over her, staring at their beautiful baby. Jackson watched her watching their lovely daughter. He was glad he met her and glad he made her his.

Simone tiptoed toward him with her shoes in one hand and a jacket in the other. Her hair was swept back. It was clear she had been running her hands through it.

"So, what's wrong?"

"Nothing." Simone shrugged, shaking her head.

She wouldn't look him in the eyes. For a split second, he felt helpless. He could not read her, as usual, and he needed to know what was on her mind.

"Come here."

Simone squinted, shaking her head. "Not tonight, baby, please."

"Come on, Simone. Come here."

Simone sighed and stared at him. He bet he could make her call his name in the end. He felt the excitement stir in the pit of his stomach. He always wanted her when she seemed least interested. He could conquer her, make her want him even when she did not want him.

Simone took a step back. "I just watched my best friend lay in what could have been her death bed. I'm mentally and emotionally exhausted and I just can't right now."

"I am not asking you to. Why can't you let me make you feel better?"

He lightly caressed the nape of her neck, watching her eyes move to his lips. She stood still, letting him tickle her special spot.

"Can't you just relax and let me make you feel better?" He pressed his finger on her special spot before leaning in to kiss it. Her eyes closed with her head reclining. Jackson had to smile. He had his wife completely open. As he should. He traced a spot around the nape of her neck, licking lightly. Simone shuddered, her shoes dropping to the floor. Jackson stood directly in front of her, not touching, letting the tension build.

"Just relax."

He unbuttoned her shirt, pushed it off her shoulders, and sunk his teeth into her neck just above her shoulder, sucking deeply. He heard a deep sigh and bit into her neck again.

"Jackson, I can't—"

"Shh!" Gently, he licked her lips, his hand stroking her breast. "Let me make love to you."

He finally put his hands on the small of her back, pulling her into him. Her frame dissolved as his imprint pressed against her. It was the best thing about his wife. She loved his penis. It was why he always felt so confident because he knew he must have been blessed with a special gift. She melted every time she touched it.

"Put your hand on it." He knew she would not complain, and she did not. He unbuckled his pants, unzipped them, and pushed her hand inside the fitted briefs. They both sighed at the same time.

"Come on." He did not want to make love to her right outside of his baby's bedroom. He led her to their room, unsnapping her pants and running his hand along her hipbone. Her hands stroked him firmly, groping him and tugging. He tried to shift and pull back because he felt himself becoming too excited too quickly. Simone stepped back and pulled her shirt completely off. She cupped her breast with one hand and stroked him with the other. He watched her, fascinated. She had never done that before.

Jackson groaned loudly. Watching her fondle her breast turned him on. The throbbing pulse tingling through his center mass was making his head spin.

"Damn, Simone."

Suddenly he felt nothing. Why was she not stroking him anymore? He glanced at her and felt his stomach drop. She had stopped grasping him as she gently stroked the tip of her temple, her fingers disappearing inside of her. She sighed, her lips parted, her hand plunged deeper into her depths as her legs parted. She opened her eyes and looked at Jackson, making eye contact with him for the first time. Then, she stopped. Jackson stared at her, his brow furrowed, his mouth opened. What the hell? When had she started this, touching and stroking herself while they were making love, like some tramp? She had stopped pleasing him, left him hanging there with a hard-on. They stared at each other, Simone's hands dropping to her side.

"What's up?"

"Nothing."

"What are you doing?"

"I...I wanted to try something different."

"Touching me wasn't enough for you?"

Simone bit her bottom lip, her face twisted in embarrassment. Jackson took her hand and placed it back on his near limp penis.

Staring into her eyes, he watched the pained expression on her face as she stroked him again. She did not want to do it. For the first time, he realized she did not want him. The more she stroked, the limper he became until she was only causing him pain. He put his hand over hers, stopping her. They were blanketed by silence and Jackson could not find any words at all. Speechless.

"What's happening?"

Simone shrugged, her bottom lip quivering.

"Are you having an affair?"

She raised her head, meeting his eyes. "Have I ever?"

"Then what is wrong with you?"

"What's wrong with me? What's wrong with you? Sex is just about you nutting off. You don't ever give a damn about me!"

The outburst shocked him, but he immediately felt enraged. He was not the selfish one, she was. How was it his fault? "Don't blame me because you can't get yours off."

"Are you kidding me?"

He stared as Simone broke into a giggling fit, which led to her laughing aloud.

"What the fuck is so funny?"

Simone tossed her head back, her laugh was hard and demon-like, as tears formed tiny streams down her face.

"What is the joke?" he yelled, succumbing to a helpless feeling.

"Us. We are the joke. Do you really believe I can't finish? That there is something wrong with me? Or is it that you are never there when I finish? Doesn't that mean there might be something wrong with—"

"Simone. I don't know whom you are doing or what is going on with you. Obviously, I don't satisfy you and, to be honest, as a wife, you don't satisfy me. So…"

She stopped laughing, the tears still rolling down her face. The smile was no longer in her eyes. She stared at him as if finally satisfied.

"So, there it is." Her mouth formed a sour grin.

He shrugged. "There it is."

Simone nodded, walked to the bathroom, and closed the door.

CHAPTER 18

S imone eyed the gasoline pump as she swiped her credit card. *There goes dinner tonight,* she thought. She had to fill up her tank, stretching out every penny. Gasoline rates were sky high and her measly bonus had not helped at all. She kept her eye on the pump, watching the numbers soar, her disappointment growing with each click of the meter. When the pump passed thirty dollars, with no signs of slowing down, she gave up watching the meter and gazed around her. On a typical sunny day in Prince George's County, Maryland, beautiful Black folks in their toy cars were pumping gas all around her. One young girl, who looked to be in high school, jumped into her two-door Mercedes Benz, with the top down and shades on. She wondered what it felt like to have folks with money.

She turned her head toward the sound of music blasting from a gray sports car. It was one of her favorite songs, a club hopper she would not dare listen to in front of her uptight husband. Jackson only listened to jazz and slow jams, which was why Simone loved days like today, when he was traveling, the baby was with her mother, and she could ride around in her SUV, windows down and hip-hop music blasting. She could let loose and remember the time before she was the prim and proper wife; when she snuck kisses behind the bleachers or danced a slow grind with her boyfriend in the middle of the dance floor.

Pushing her shades up on top of her head, she noticed the light-brown face in the driver's seat of the sports car. Not realizing she was staring until the man behind the wheel smiled, Simone jumped as the nozzle in her hand clicked. She replaced the nozzle on the pump, screwed the cap on the gas tank, careful not to look in the direction of the smiling man, and reached for a paper towel from the dispenser. Quickly climbing into her Lexus NX, Simone noticed she needed to clean her windshield. She climbed back out, and, keeping her eyes lowered, located the squeegee.

"Simone?"

Simone turned suddenly to see the light brown man standing behind her. *Damn.* Her heart rate quickened as she stood next to such a beautiful man.

"Simone, right?"

"Yeah." Simone smiled, looking directly into his eyes for the first time. *Pull yourself together, girl, he is young enough to be your baby brother.* He looked familiar. "Don't I know you?"

"You don't remember me? Darius Winfield. I used to play football with—"

"Terrance." The corner of her mouth turned up into a seductive smirk. *Of course. Damn. Who would've thought you could grow into two hundred plus pounds of masculine wonderland? Keep your eyes focused on his neck and face, girl, don't look down at his chest. Or his feet.* She cleared her throat. "Of course, I remember you."

They looked at each other for an awkward second, and then he stepped toward her, arms opened for a friendly hug, which she normally would have offered first had he not been so gorgeous. She silently chastised herself for not relaxing and, dropping the squeegee to the ground, she stepped into his embrace, careful not to fully caress him.

"So how is Terrance? What is he up to?"

"Still playing. This is his redshirt senior year at Duke University." She picked up the squeegee and placed it back into the pail. "What about you?"

"Pro. Four years ago."

"Of course, I knew that. Congratulations. I am losing time, or it's going by too fast. Terrance went to the draft party, right?"

"Yeah, man, it was huge. Kind of like a dream. Then, anyway. Real life now."

"I am so proud of you. We watch you, you know. I just haven't seen you in person in so long or without a helmet, that it took me a moment."

"You watch the games?"

Well, not really. Jackson always watched, she only checked in long enough to see him do something, to cheer on her brother's friend, the little boy who had the cute little crush on her.

"Naw, I just watch you." She shrugged and smiled.

"Aw, still no patience for football, huh?"

They laughed.

"So, is that your car?"

"Yep. Taking the Maserati for a spin."

"So, how is this life? Is it everything you dreamed of? You always talked about being famous, making millions."

"Yeah, it's good. I can't complain. I like not being famous, though. Get to play and live life. A lot of stress. And the expectations are bizarre. I can't believe how important the little things are and how no one seems to care about what matters."

She nodded in agreement. She knew all too well. Sometimes she felt like she was suffering, drowning under a lake of expectations. They stared at each other.

"So, if I recall, you married Jackson Woodson, right?" Scanning her figure, he slowly shook his head and bit the inside of his mouth. "You're actually married, huh?"

Simone nodded woodenly. "Yeah, the wedding was the same week as your party. That's why I missed it."

"Yeah, I remember. How is married life treating you?"

Her smile faded as she looked away from him. "I can't complain, I guess."

He observed her. She knew she should have given a more enthusiastic answer, but she simply could not muster excitement over something dead.

"Well," she dragged out. "I better get going. It was wonderful seeing you. You should keep in touch."

The look in his eyes changed slightly. She suddenly became flushed. She had not meant for it to come out like that, so throaty. She meant to keep it light, to say that he should keep in touch with Terrance.

"I mean, you and Terrance were really close and, you know, *we* would like to see you."

He smiled, but his eyes remained locked on hers. "Yeah, I will. Keep in touch with you…Terrance." They stared at each other for another moment. "It was good seeing you, Mrs. Woodson."

Her married name. Realizing he never called her that before today, she confirmed, "Simone. Still Simone."

"Simone," he said much softer. "It was good seeing you, Simone."

"Okay, well, you take care of yourself." This time she took the step closer for the friendly departing hug. This time, there was no space between them. She inhaled his scent, closed her eyes, and smiled.

He took a couple of steps backward, his eyes still on her. Then he smiled and turned toward his car.

Simone flipped the sunglasses down onto her face and climbed in her SUV. Her hands were shaking, and she felt flushed. How long had it been since someone looked at her in that way? Looked at her as if they wanted to devour her. She could not remember.

Stop it. He is a child. If he was a year or two older than her little brother, then he was at least eight years her junior. *He's just flirting to see if he can get away with it. To test how many folks turn groupie now that he is a pro football player. Stop tripping.*

She started her engine to pull out of the gas station. As she waited for traffic to clear for her to turn right, the Maserati pulled up alongside her.

"Simone!"

She saw his mouth moving, but could not hear him.

"Huh?"

He smiled, shaking his head, and motioned for her to roll down the window.

Laughing at herself, she rolled down the window.

"Simone, I was just thinking, are you busy?"

"No. Not really."

"Have you ever ridden in a Maserati before?"

She bit her lip, trying to control the smile invading her face.

"So, where should we go?"

Simone shrugged, trying to keep her grin from becoming a full smile. He asked her to ride. She knew it did not mean anything, the old player in her remembering the rules of the game. Still, it felt good for a handsome man to invite her to join him. She enjoyed parking her car in the crowded lot and climbing into the low, wide car. It felt damn good to watch his eyes take in the full width of her and grin appreciatively as he held her hand and commented on her curly hair. She did not care where they went.

"Wherever you take me."

He gazed at her, the smile in his eyes contained a sensuous flame. Though difficult to take his eyes off her, he did and eased the car out of the parking lot. "Let's go where there are some empty roads. Open this baby up a bit."

"Cool."

He turned the music down and they rode in silence.

"I hope you don't mind my asking you to ride."

"Not at all."

"Good. I didn't want you to be offended or anything."

"Why would I be offended?"

He looked down at her hand. Her wedding band. She had allowed herself to forget about it. Temporarily.

He shrugged. "I don't know. I just wasn't sure, now that you're married. I always liked being around you."

Simone's breath caught in her throat. Either he was the sincerest man she had ever met or he had serious game. "That's sweet."

"No, it's true."

They rode in silence until they reached a huge strip of highway with light traffic.

"Here we go!"

Bracing herself, Simone felt the power of the automobile captivate her. They sped down the highway and she opened up with laughter, encouraged him to floor it, then closed her eyes and pretended she was flying and floating. Thrilled, Simone released all inhibitions.

She opened her eyes when she felt the car slowing to normal speed. He was watching her, glancing between her and the road.

"What do you think?"

"Damn." Simone smiled widely.

"Yep, that's what's up."

As she laughed, he watched her. She was radiant. The curve of her pouty lips enticed him. He wanted to kiss them. Married or not, he wanted her.

"So, you got some time on your hands, or do I have to get you back?"

"I've got a little time. Why?"

"Want to get some lunch?"

"Definitely."

He turned off the main route onto a side road and followed it to a burger diner.

Simone waited in the car while he went in, and her mind flipped into full throttle, as she held a full conversation with herself. "What am I doing here? This is nothing. He is just grown, knows how to have a lady friend. Just being friendly. That's all. Why am I tripping? He's just a friend. A friend of my brother's. That's it. Nothing more. Nothing less. But damn, he sure is—stop it, Simone. Just stop it!"

She spotted him approaching with the tray and climbed out of the car. They chose the picnic table in the rear, away from other diners. She sat next to him, their backs to the diner, facing the thick grove of trees.

"I love French fries."

"Looks like you love ketchup, too."

"Yep." She smiled, squeezing a mound of ketchup onto the tray. "For dipping only. Never pour it all over the fries."

"It's a science, right?" He watched while she dipped the hot French fry and ate it. "You know, I have always liked you."

"I've always liked you, too," Simone said easily through a mouthful of food.

"Naw." Darius sat the burger on the tray. "I have always *wanted* you."

Simone squared her shoulders. Now that was a little too forward. What was she supposed to say to that? She looked at the tray of food and the mound of ketchup, anything to avoid eye contact.

"Didn't you know?"

She glanced up at him. "You had a crush. All boys go through that. I knew you would outgrow it."

"It wasn't a crush."

"Of course, it was. What else could it have been?"

"I loved you. I was in love." He smiled, shakily, but his eyes never blinked. "There was nothing I could do about it, but I loved you."

"Well, it happens to us all. That deep infatuation stuff. Then you don't see the person for a few weeks, forget all about them—"

"I didn't forget. I never forgot you. It wasn't just infatuation. I was in love." He stared at her for a few minutes.

As much as she tried, she could not break away from his gaze. It reminded her of how he used to look at her when she would pick him and Terrance up and escort them to wherever they needed to go. Since she was the older sister with an apartment, she was always Terrance's escape route.

She was a loyal sister, willingly ready to take them on their next adventure.

She remembered how he used to look at her then, actually stared at her, getting tongue-tied in her presence. Even Terrance joked about it when Darius was not around. She thought it was cute, even funny. She would purposely flirt with him to watch him stutter and blush, watch his caramel-colored face blush.

Now she was the one blushing. Her deep brown skin suddenly felt hot as she imagined what his lips would taste like, how she would love to straddle him and feel his rise against her temple. Still, she could not do that. He was her little brother's friend. What would he think of her? What if he told?

He caressed the small of her back. "I still am."

Her mouth fell open. He leaned in and kissed her lightly on the forehead, then the tip of her nose. Blood rushed to her head and warmth flooded her core. Her eyelids felt heavy, her mind dizzy. She wanted him. As bizarre as it sounded, she wanted him, but she was married with a child. Besides, she was easily eight years older.

With his forehead against hers, he closed his eyes. "I am not asking you for forever. I know you have…obligations. We have now."

"Then what? There is too much at stake."

"There is nothing at stake because this stays between us. We both have something to lose. I just don't want to lose another opportunity to be near you. To make something I thought about daily come true."

Daily? Imagine that. Even if it were not true, his approach felt so romantic and poetic that she hoped he would kiss her again. Not wanting to speak, she wanted to feel the sudden flood of desire overtake her again.

He planted a light kiss on her neck. The feel of his head between her shoulder and neck made her shudder, sending a rush of chills throughout her. *My, my, my,* was the only thought she could gather.

After a long pause, he bit down on his lip. "I want to be with you." His lips graced her ear. "Do you want me, Simone?"

"Yes." She spoke lower than a whisper. So low, he barely heard her.

"Tell me you want me. I need to hear it."

"I want you. Now," she whispered, amazed at how quickly she had lost control.

He kissed her neck again while his index finger slowly traced a path down the V-neckline of her shirt and circled the base of her breast. With her eyes closed, she placed her hand on his thigh. His fingers lingered in front of her for a second. She sighed as she enjoyed the sensation of his finger lightly stroking her hardened nipple protruding through her shirt. Her hand firmly grasped his thigh, running slowly along the ridge to his tight, rippled stomach. The continuous waves of pleasure from his hand stroking her breast caused a moan to escape her, just as he fully covered her lips with his, his tongue lightly teasing hers, in and out, just enough to leave her breathless in anticipation.

The first kisses were slow, lingering, and playful. As the waves of passion continued to crash against her inner shore, the kiss became more passionate, deeper, her mouth wide open.

He lowered his hand from her breast, squeezing her knee then her thigh, before slipping his hand under her denim skirt. He massaged her inner thigh, stopping just at the tip of her panties and rubbing lightly. He pressed against her with his thumb, and she moaned softly, leaning into him.

Separating himself from her for a moment, Darius glanced around. Far away from the other few customers, their table slightly visible beneath the low swinging branches. He swung one leg over the bench and pulled her into him, her back pressed against his chest, his right arm around her. From afar, it appeared they were merely sitting close, embracing. As his left hand reached under her shirt and lightly palmed her lace-covered breast, he kissed the back of her neck, while he slid his other hand into the cup of her bra, firmly cupping her full breast, rubbing her nipple between his forefinger and thumb. She grasped his thigh firmly as she moaned in delight.

"Will you let me make love to you?"

Simone nodded, wondering what happened to her resolve, to her ability to decline his offer. She shouldn't do this, but the memory of his young, raw admiration amazed her. She could still see it in his eyes. He thought she was beautiful and she could see a wonderful reflection of herself in him. Darius looked at her like a man in love when every part of his woman is enhanced, magnified, and fulfilled. She wanted to lose herself in that image, in that raw, unadulterated admiration.

"I have waited to make love to you for years," he whispered against the back of her neck, before gently sucking it.

As he sucked her neck, his hand left her breast and gently pressed against her belly, submerging under the waistline of her skirt and panties, firmly cupping the ridge of her pelvis. As she leaned back a little, a slight shudder passed through her again, and he submerged his fingers into the depths of her ocean. Still sitting sideways, his left arm hidden from view, he massaged and stroked the swelling knot between her labia, kissing her neck through her moans and gasps, gingerly balancing her frame against his. She rocked slightly in response to the rhythm of his fingers, plunging deep inside of her, while his thumb continued to press against her bud.

"Do you like that?"

She nodded, unable to form her mouth to make a plausible statement; his fingers moved expertly around her temple, in and out of her, up and down, teasing her inner walls and driving her into a delirious state.

His fingers stopped moving, and he whispered again, "Do you like that?"

"Don't stop."

As his focus returned to her pleasure zone, she squeezed his thigh, trying with all her power not to scream, as she felt wave after wave of pleasure wash over her. Then, she was completely exhausted. She nestled back against his chest, while his fingers continued to play.

"Simone."

"Hmm." She hoped he would not say something that would ruin this moment, ruin this feeling of complete relaxation.

"How do you feel?"

She smiled and shook her head. She was not ready to talk yet.

"I have thought about how to please you for years."

Opening her eyes, she turned looked up at him. Their eyes connected. She saw love there, although it frightened her. She would not focus on it, would not acknowledge it. She did not want to ruin this moment.

Simone had never been stroked into orgasm by a man before, had never met a man who knew how to apply just the right amount of pressure, who knew how to respond to every movement and gentle rock, how to bring her to ecstasy with only his fingers. He continued to rub her thighs, her belly and her breasts as his hand traveled lightly up and down her clothes. The now cold food sat untouched, but the look in his eyes was ravenous.

"Come home with me."

Without hesitation, she accepted his invitation.

CHAPTER 19

⟨❋⟩⟲

They never made it to his house. Sitting in the Maserati, he continued to rub her thigh. She simply wanted to accept it and to bask in the attention. She also wanted to please him, to return some of what she felt. She climbed over the center console and straddled him, pressing against him as she pressed the control that lowered the seat.

"Oh, God."

His utterance surprised her. For the first time, he seemed scared and nervous. She looked deeply into his eyes as she gingerly kissed each lip, and then traced the fullness of his lips with her tongue. Yes, he was nervous, all right, but not apprehensive, as he stared at her questioningly. At first, she did not understand it, could not figure out how someone so astute could now seem on edge.

"What's wrong?" she whispered, nose-to-nose with him. "Did I do something?"

"No, it's just—" He sighed deeply, and she understood. This meant something to him. This was special. That tenderness, that admission of weakness spawned the strongest feeling of caring she had ever felt toward anyone.

"It will be all right," she whispered.

She kissed him, slowly and deeply. He wrapped his arms around her torso, his broad frame enveloping her, his hand resting lightly on the back of her head. With each kiss, she rhythmically pressed against him, rocking her pelvis against his, feeling his thick rise through the light gym shorts he wore.

Simone nibbled on his neck, ran her hands up and down the back of his head, and kissed him deeply as she continued her slow, methodic grind, something she never did with Jackson. Darius moaned thickly and held her tightly, his hands resting on her hips as she gyrated over his pelvis.

"Oh, God," he uttered again, this time closing his eyes and giving himself over to the pressure of her hovering over his penis, her hips rotating, her breasts rubbing up and down his torso. "I can't take it."

"Shhh." Simone continued becoming familiar as she ran her hands down his torso and he raised his hips slightly, allowing her to lower his shorts.

"Condom?"

Darius opened his eyes, seemingly unable to move as Simone planted her knees in the side of the seat and lifted her hips, allowing her to stroke him with both hands. He reached under the seat, and Simone heard a compartment click and heard the tearing of the small packet. Taking it from him, she rolled it onto his penis. Kissing him deeply, she raised her hips and slowly lowered herself onto him, hearing him gasp and moan. When she fully enveloped him, she resumed kissing him and gyrating, barely lifting her hips. He filled her up to her core; like a hand in glove, he was the perfect fit.

After a few minutes, her passion took over and she could no longer contain herself. Leaning completely on him, her hands gripping the headrest, she lifted and lowered herself, enjoying the complete fullness of his girth. Whenever she lowered herself, she would gyrate and grind her hips, rubbing her fleshy pearl against his shaft. She continued this until they were both lost in the sensuous wave of the motion. He held onto her hips as he climaxed, jerking and grabbing, sighing and moaning, making an ugly, yet satisfied, face.

They lay in the Maserati for a long time until she was able to peel herself from his arms. He bathed her in kisses, whispered repeated promises of ecstasy, and finally, they separated and he drove slowly to his house.

CHAPTER 20

S
he washed every inch and crevice of her body three times. The house was spotless. Jackson was due home any second, and they planned to spend the rest of the weekend together before going to pick up the baby. She looked forward to it before, hoping she could be clever enough to seduce him, to get him to pay attention and want to make love. Lately, he always seemed so tired. All he spoke of was his obligations at work, the different things he was counting on to make money so they would be comfortable. However, they were already comfortable and Simone felt bored. Well, she had been bored, before the last twenty-four hours with Darius.

Simone harbored no guilt. None at all. She enjoyed every minute of Darius and wished the day and night would never end. Nevertheless, there she stood, waiting for her husband to return, waiting for her mundane life to resume.

"Hey, honey."

She was not expecting the sound of his voice. The deep, reliable, rich tone brought on the flood of guilt. Her knees caved a little. "Get it together," she said to herself. "There is nothing you can do now. It's over." Simone hurried downstairs to greet her husband.

"Hi, Jackson. How was your trip?"

"All right. Did you miss me?"

"Yep. Of course."

"I called all night. You didn't answer."

"Dead battery. Just recharged this morning. Sorry about that."

"Well, I called the house phone, too."

"Did you?" Simone picked up his bag and headed for their bedroom. "I don't know how I missed that." She placed the bag on the bed. "I needed a little solitude anyway, so I didn't have it near me."

He nodded, following her into the bedroom. He observed her closely. "You look nice."

"Thanks." She fluttered past him to unpack his bag, placing his toiletries in the bathroom.

"I missed you."

Uh oh. It was his tone. The *once-every-blue-moon-I-want-to-get-it-on* tone. No. She did not want to do that. She could not have sex with him after making love to Darius every which way for the past twenty-four hours. She simply would not do it.

"I missed you, too," she forced through clenched teeth as he moved closer to her for a kiss. She turned her head before he made contact, landing a peck on her cheek.

"Come here, let me have some."

Which was exactly why he was getting none. Jackson had no romance, no sense of adventure. No foreplay, no excitement. Just a "let me have some" mentality.

"I don't feel well, Jackson. I'm sorry." Simone floated out of the room to get the other bags to help him unpack.

❦

It had been twelve days since her encounter. Simone tried to resume a normal life, but she found it hard to do. The thought of Darius's touch, his taste, his smell consumed her mind, making it impossible to focus on the slightest tasks. She had not made love to Jackson. Nor did she plan to. Although she felt guilty about giving herself to another man, the guilt was caused by her disappointment that she could no longer consider herself the perfect wife. It was not an overwhelming loss for going outside of her marriage. Jackson could be so cold, so stiff; if Simone sought warmth somewhere else, she could not be blamed.

As Simone returned from her kickboxing class, she noticed the voicemail message on her cell phone. She rarely checked voicemail. Those who knew her knew not to waste time leaving a message. She checked the caller ID. No name appeared with the number. She kicked off her sneakers and stretched out across the bed, calling the voicemail. It took a few times to remember the password.

"I miss you. I am sorry. I know I shouldn't do this. Can we have one mo' 'gain?"

She could not believe Darius had left such a message. She could have been busted. What the hell was he thinking? Yet, in the next second, she giggled wildly, a euphoric pleasure spread through her. He wanted to see her again. Be with her again. Hold up! Was that a booty call?

She replayed the message, listening to the inflections in his voice. It did not matter. She wanted to see him again. When and how? Why? It was only a one-time thing, a perfect opportunity at a perfect time. Anything more would be an affair. Besides, she did not want an affair. Sneaking out at all times to steal a few minutes here and there, always risking exposure. It was not the lifestyle she wanted to live. No, she wasn't going to do that. Just one more time.

As she checked the driveway to make sure Jackson had not returned, she called the unidentified number.

"You got my message?"

"What, no hello? No, how are you?"

"*Como esta, sexy mami?*" His baritone voice made her smile and her heart tingle.

"*Esta bien.*" The mere sound of his voice gave her joy. Her vagina was responding, and she had not been on the phone for five minutes.

"So, when can I see you again?"

"I don't know. It depends on what you have in mind."

"You. I have in mind."

She sighed deeply, enjoying his voice.

"Tomorrow. I want to have you for lunch."

"Excuse me."

"Over for lunch. Can you come over at lunchtime?"

"I don't know."

There was silence for a few minutes while she weighed the advantages over the risk. Jasmine would be in childcare and Jackson would be at work. If she were careful…

"Please!"

Hearing him plead broke any strength she had. "Yeah. Tomorrow at lunch. Text me your address." She would give this man anything he wanted.

That evening, Jackson asked about her day and planned the next day's events and expectations. She finished the dishes, nodding and busying herself with cleaning, but her every thought was of Darius.

CHAPTER 21

D arius met her at the door before she could ring the bell. As she reached for the huge knocker, one of the massive, double doors swung open and he pulled her into him, hugging her close, his tongue exploring her mouth.

She squealed in surprise but was quickly lost in the urgency of his passion.

He moved her against the wall, pressing her between the cold smooth surface and his hard, huge physique. He rubbed up and down her torso while he deeply kissed her, tearing away from her mouth and planting kisses around her neck. Her eyes closed, her mouth opened, she felt on fire. With his hand, he easily brushed away the cloth of her blouse, his mouth landing intently on her breast. Kissing and sucking each breast, while massaging the other, she called out his name in pleasure.

"Baby," he moaned. "Say my name again."

She did, repeating with so much passion, while he separated her thighs with his knee.

When he entered her, they both groaned in pleasure, their eyes locked on one another. She could feel every inch of his girth as if her insides were swollen and fitting against the perfect shape of him. She shouted in pleasure as he seemed to grow inside of her, while he rocked back and forth forcefully. Pushing back her legs, he adjusted his thrust, connecting with her G-spot. She screamed uncontrollably until her body spasmed and he finally released, his shouts drowning her out. That was the best sex she had ever had in her life! She basked in the afterglow of Darius, as they lay quietly on the floor.

He lifted her and carried her to his bedroom. She kept her eyes closed and remained silent. That he could lift her, carry her as if she were the lightest thing in the world, meant everything to her. She was not a burden, someone to be overlooked and mistreated when the opportunity arose. He viewed her as a beautiful, blooming flower rather than burdensome.

Simone spent the rest of the afternoon, and early that evening, wrapped in his arms, enjoying safety and peace. They made love all afternoon, allowing him full access to her mind and body. She was beyond a one-night stand. She no longer had control.

❦

"Why didn't you call to tell me dinner was going to be late?"

"Because, Jackson, dinner was the last thing on my mind."

"Well, what is on your mind? It damn sure ain't me or us."

"What?" She placed the pan of baked pork chops on the island. "What the hell is that supposed to mean?"

"It means I shouldn't have to wait for dinner after a hard day's work."

Simone remained silent and thought, *A hard day's work, my ass.* How hard was managing other people's money? "I work, too, you know, Jackson."

"Your damn mind has been somewhere else lately. That's all I am saying. I don't understand your problem."

"I don't have a problem, Jackson."

"Well, then what's going on with you?"

"Nothing. Maybe the fact that you are just now tuning in—after three years of my requests for a partner in this relationship—leads you to believe something is wrong."

She lowered a plate from the shelf and piled a healthy heaping of food onto it.

"I don't need that much food. Don't overreact."

"Jackson, I am not overreacting. I am not being irrational. What I am is completely pissed off that you would have the nerve to criticize me when you act like you don't even know me for weeks at a time."

Simone ached from the lovemaking escapade earlier that day. She and Darius had been seeing each other at least once a week for the past two months. She craved him. She knew she was addicted, but she did not want rehab. Darius studied her every movement, her every response, and played her as if she were a finely tuned instrument. The slightest blow from his sweet lips could send her into euphoria.

Jackson was the farthest thing from her mind. She had not thought about him at all. He'd noticed.

A small part of her panicked. Simone realized her comfortable existence was, in large part, due to his efforts. However, she also wanted to feel loved and protected and Jackson never provided her that kind of security.

"Simone, what's going on with you? You can leave. I won't fight you."

Simone stared at him. "Are you threatening me? What are you talking about?"

"No. This is me saying that something's up."

"Yeah, you never pay me any attention. All you care about is the bills, your job, getting some sleep—"

"Listen to you. You sound like a spoiled brat. 'Nobody ever treats me like I want,'" he mimicked her with disgust.

Simone stared at the back of his head, wondering whether she should leave him or not. She searched for an answer. After carefully sitting the plate on the countertop, she removed her apron and walked quietly to her bedroom. "You son of a bitch," she mumbled under her breath.

CHAPTER 22

⸻❦⸻

The hotel lobby was tiled in fine marble, making India's red-bottom, stiletto pumps echo with each step. Chandeliers of all sizes hung from the domed, Romanesque-painted ceiling, at least one hundred feet high. Embroidered silk sofas surrounded a large, flat-screen television. The twin doors leading into the lobby were a pristine white with golden handles. The desk was made of amber-colored wood and a green granite top. Exquisite paintings hung from the rich, red walls. Even the door hinges were engraved with swirls and elegant designs.

India pulled up next to Jackson, as he sat at a corner table in the lounge of the Beauregard Hotel in Boston, Massachusetts, and sat across the table from him.

Jackson nodded at her presence and sipped the cognac. "I loathe these conferences."

India ignored his complaining and got straight to the point. "You need to get an attorney."

"No. The firm is supporting me right now. I think they can handle it."

India sighed, shaking her head. "You really don't know this game, huh?"

"Why don't you break it down for me?" Jackson had not meant to be so sarcastic. He watched her facial expression as she considered him. She did not have to help him at all.

Who would have thought an office assistant would have so much knowledge? However, as it turned out, India was a licensed paralegal who was attending evening law school at Georgetown University Law Center. She was a more valuable resource than he could have ever imagined. Jackson also found her to be beautiful. The more they talked and the more she helped, the more attractive she became to him. He could trust her. She felt so reliable and calm. The last thing he wanted to do was to offend her.

"The game is simple. It is designed for a white man's success. An exception will be allowed for you if you make them enough money. If you get in the way, stop earning dollars, or worse yet, require them to spend money, then you are out of the game. Checkmate."

"Well, I am making them money."

"No. They are breaking even with what you make and what a white boy, doing the same job, would make. The minority thing was a plus in that respect, proof of their professed liberal stance. This sexual harassment thing..." she paused, in deep thought. She wiggled her finger. "It could scar their reputation, costing them clients and business. That's millions. If they have to defend you, that's thousands in legal fees lost. If they simply quieted her by firing you and giving her a payoff or another job, now you're talking a simple, affordable solution."

Jackson reclined in his seat, breathing hard. He did not like to think of himself as expendable. He had busted his ass over the last several years, trying to convince himself and them that he was irreplaceable. However, he knew better.

India continued, eyebrows raised and lips pursed. "The firm is saying they will handle it. That means they will look out for *their* best interest. Don't think a deal can't and won't be made that would protect them and place liability solely on you. In the end, their representation means just that. Someone to represent the firm's interest."

"Damn it! Why is this thing even going this far?"

"Well, that's why you need your own attorney. They should have been able to make this go away a while ago. You've got to wonder why it didn't."

"Yeah, why didn't it?" He glanced at her through red eyes. "Thanks, India, for coming out. I mean, you have helped me so much and I know it's risky."

"I have seen this set up a million times before. They get rid of us a few ways. For the attorneys, they always go to the writing thing. Like clockwork. First, they find the writing questionable, then the workload lightens, less billable hours… well, you know."

Jackson nodded. Even he had noticed it. The only ones blindsided were the young, Black attorneys; too much pride, and too much riding on the line to admit they were in trouble or to ask for help. He had watched many leave the same way. He was not as good as India. He had watched without lifting a finger, hoping he would be seen differently.

"For you guys, it's different. The moneymen. Everyone wants to keep you happy and loyal until you become a liability." She nodded. "Trust me, Nina knows the game, and she knew exactly how to play it. She knew to paint you as a liability to the firm."

"I messed with the wrong one."

"Hell, yeah you did."

They glanced at each other and smiled. That was what he liked about her. She could play it so straitlaced, but keep it real when she needed to, regardless of his position over her. It made him want her more. She was special and completely off-limits. She appeared uninterested in him in that way, and she made sure to mention his wife whenever the territory felt unsure. Still, she sat with him and advised him. He appreciated it.

"So, do you have anyone in mind?"

"Of course. You need to contact this sister." She handed a black business card to him that was trimmed in solid, light pink with the information in raised, gray lettering shadowed by pink. T. Lynn Taylor. "A Black woman lawyer immediately changes the tone, takes away some assumptions that you are biased against the Black woman, or are a womanizer. This woman is bad. Five-grand retainer."

He grimaced.

"Please," she laughed lightly, "you better cough that money up without so much as a blink. She is going to have to hardball with both Nina's people and the firm. You need to make the call today."

"How do you know her?"

"We were…close."

What the hell did that mean? Jackson stared at India. Was she gay? He did not think so. She did not give out a gay vibe. He raised an eyebrow, and she smiled.

"I am sure you would like to know, but I am not going there with you. Not today."

"Come on, how do you know her?"

"Listen. This is what you need to know. She is a Hoya Lawya. Well-connected. Was a solo practitioner for seven years. Law firm absorbed her and made her an equity partner in the deal."

"She's like that?"

"Yeah. She's like that. Her normal retainer is ten thousand or outrageous hourly fees. I already told her the situation. She might not be the friendliest toward you, but she will get your ass out of a bind."

"I'll call her immediately."

"One more thing. The clerk sent over the itinerary and information request for the preliminary meeting between Nina's rep and the firm. The thing is…" India sighed, looking around. Her face became deadly serious, her eyes locked on Jackson. "I am not supposed to reveal this to you. I will deny this conversation ever happened."

"Understood."

"Well, the thing is, they requested the name and contact information for all of your previous assistants. The firm didn't fight it."

Jackson closed his eyes and clenched his fists. That was what he did not want to hear. "It's gotten that far already?"

"Yep. Already."

"I need to talk to Simone." He watched India as she nodded and gave him a serious look.

Standing, with her arms folded across her chest, India peered down and scolded, "Jackson, that talk should have happened a month ago," before abruptly leaving the table.

India was right. That talk should have happened a month ago. However, a week ago, Jackson had told his wife she no longer satisfied him as a woman. What a thing to say. It was the only response he had to the pain he felt. He was not enough for her; she removed her hand to touch herself. He speculated in the past, knowing she touched herself in the middle of the night while he slept. He thought it was her way of hurting him. He never thought she simply enjoyed it, enough to do it while she was with him. He knew it should not have been that big of a deal, but for him it was. What type of woman was she after all? He felt like the world he created was cracking and falling away in big chunks.

Jackson needed to hear Simone's voice. Tonight. He hated being on travel right now. Normally, travel offered a great relief from her. From the obligations of her. From the silent treatment. From the heavy blame and the thick tension. Even that meant she was at least somewhere around and he was on her mind. Yet, this time she was alone, and he felt sure he was not on her mind at all. She had not spoken to him after he told her she no longer satisfied him, but it was different. This time it did not feel like she was not speaking to him in an attempt to get his attention. No, this time she had literally cut him out of her span of acknowledgment. She went about her day, unfazed and unaffected. Unworried. When he would walk into the room, she would look up, notice him, and go on with whatever she was doing. She never asked for an explanation. Never requested an apology. Never seemed to give a damn he thought she was not satisfying.

Still, he wanted to hear her voice. Jackson called the house. The phone rang and rang. *Maybe she knows it's me, that's why she isn't answering,* he thought, as he kept calling. *Where could she be at one in the morning?* He tried her cell phone. If she answered it, he would hit the roof. *Where the hell would she be, to answer the cell and not the house phone?* He kept getting her voicemail.

She's with another man. He knew it. She was cheating. It all made sense. It answered all the questions. A very basic explanation. She could touch herself while making love to him, thinking of her lover's touch. She could exist without worrying about him because some other man was licking her pearl, sucking her breasts, and stroking her G-spot. His mind's eye played it like a broken movie projector: her hair pushed back, the wide smile on her face, eyes barely opened, enough to watch the euphoric energy her inner svelte lining made flow through any man. She had velvet pussy, and she loved the feel of dick, which instantly made her velvet feel like it was covered in satin. No man would give that up. Who would deny himself the pure joy of a woman who loved sexing for the simple sake of sexing?

"Son of a—" He squeezed the back of his neck.

It was typical. When his whole world was crumbling, it was just like Simone to add to his problems. Not like a real wife who would be there to support him, forgive him and help him to move forward. No, while his career was in jeopardy, his wife was having some type of love affair.

Jackson stared at the television. "Fuck this," he muttered. He yanked the investigator's number out of his wallet. He was getting to the bottom of this. Tonight.

Jackson chewed on his bottom lip as the phone rang.

"Jackson? What's wrong?"

"Martia, I know it's late. I got another issue."

"I'm on the first one. She is playing it clean. Her attorney prepped her, but if there is any dirt, you know I will find it."

"I know." Jackson suddenly felt embarrassed. He had used Martia for digging up dirt he threw in people's faces to make them go away quietly. To protect his life. Now, the dirt was on him, the stain across his marriage. He hated to admit it.

"You still there? What else do you need?"

"Nothing. I, uh, well…I am going to hire an attorney on this current thing. She might want to see your results, too."

"No problem. Good move. Forward her info, send me an email, and I will let you know what I know before I talk with her, though. That's how I operate. You are still my client, not her."

"Thanks, Martia."

"Jackson, you know I don't judge. I am discreet. If you need anything else, please let me know."

He paused, wondering how she knew his hesitation. Probably from years of experience.

"I will. Thank you."

"No problem."

CHAPTER 23

I t was supposed to end after the third visit. She should not be here. She was pushing her luck, and they both knew it. Why didn't she have the willpower to cut it off weeks ago? Simone lay flat on her back across the middle of Darius's king-sized bed. The sunlight streamed across the room, its rays warming her forehead, her chest, and the top of her thighs. Simone sighed, wondering where Darius had gone while she slept.

Shifting, she draped her arm over her eyes, blocking the sunshine. She had to end this. There was no other choice. The picture of the woman on his dresser was evidence of that. He had another life, too, and a love. Discovery could ruin just as much for him as her. The woman was so pretty. Why would he want her, with her baggage, her stretch marks and extra weight, her uncertainty? He wanted this as much as she had wanted it—a simple, one-night stand to release long-awaited lust. Yet, he claimed love at every turn.

Simone wished he would not say it. She did not know how to respond or what she should say. If she answered with love, then what would be the next step? Would there be no next step, simply two secret lovers living double lives? Again, Simone glanced at the picture. The woman was cinnamon brown with a flawless weave, skintight dress, and pure beauty. Why had she not noticed the picture before? Too busy getting her groove on.

She heard his footsteps approaching the room. She knew his sound, the steady, even pressure of his balanced body against the hardwood floors. For the first time, she wondered how she looked in the black lace bra. Nowhere near as flawless and toned as Miss Picture. Simone's breasts were protruding out of the cups from when Darius had held them earlier. She realized her lower half was exposed in the sunlight. Although most of their meetings had been during the daylight, she suddenly felt self-conscious. Simone lifted the bra cups over her breast and covered her waist with the sheet just as Darius darkened the threshold.

"Don't cover up. I wanted to see you." His voice made her smile, made a distinct joy swell within her chest, a feeling she had never felt before.

"You've already seen me." She smiled, not looking at him, but staring at the ceiling and then returning her arm over her eyes. She needed to say these words to put this thing to an end, and she could not do that while talking to him. "We… we need to talk."

"I know."

It had never occurred to her he might want to end it as well. Suddenly, she did not want to talk anymore, did not want to hear what he might have to say. The words from her lips made sense. From his lips, they would rip her soul to shreds. She felt sudden warmth on her thighs and lower stomach. Removing her arm, she looked down. Darius stood at the foot of the bed, washing her with a warm, soapy cloth and rinsing her with another damp cloth. His eyes remained focused on her thighs and hips as the suds covered her lower body and he gently moved his hands in circular motions.

"Darius…"

He glanced at her and grinned. "Let me finish. Then we'll talk."

Thick lather covered her lower half, her legs slightly parted and raised at the knee. Darius dropped the rinsing cloth. He caressed her hips with his hands, massaging her skin with the soap that covered her. Simone softly moaned, her eyes rolling upward. As she sighed, his hands inched along her torso, spreading the thick suds, now familiar with every inch of her.

"Look at that smile," he muttered, causing her to look at him. "That's what I wanted to see. You look like an angel when I'm touching you." He raised the warm, rinsing cloth and gently wiped away the soap. He dipped the soft towel in the bowl of warm water next to him, squeezing the water and wiping her clean. Then the thick soft cloth gently touched her skin, drying it softly.

What other emotion could it be but love that would make a man hand wash her for absolutely no reason? He probably did love her, or loved their situation. Would he not find her less attractive if the thrill of the cheating were not involved?

Feeling the bed move, Simone watched him lay his lean, athletic body across the bed, ignoring the dampness of the sheet from her impromptu wash, resting his head against her inner thigh.

"What do you want to talk about?"

The words tickled the soft skin around her jewel as he spoke. He inhaled her. She really did not want to talk anymore. She did not want him to break her heart. How many more visits did they have? How much time before she would have to go back to life without him, if she could bare it?

"You. Me. This."

"This…" He sighed, turning his head slightly to kiss her inner thigh. "You mean this?"

"No. I mean, the woman in the picture, this. Why can't I stop this, this?"

"The woman in what picture?"

Simone pointed to the dresser and Darius rose up and looked at the picture. He shook his head. She wished he had not moved. She loved the feel of his head between her thighs.

"I meant to move that."

"You shouldn't have to. I don't have any right to expect it. I am not questioning you about it. I just didn't realize that you…have someone."

He did not answer at first and his silence felt like a knot in Simone's chest.

"We have been together for a little over a year."

"You're in love?"

"I love her."

Simone sighed, covering her eyes with her arm. Tears were forming, and she needed to find a way to hide them.

Darius took a deep breath. "I am *in love* with you."

"You can't be."

He laughed aloud. "I can't be? Well, fuck it, because I am."

"I am, too."

"You're in love with you, too?"

She laughed, feeling an easy contentment spread through her as he returned his head to kiss her other thigh. "I am in love with you, too."

"So now what?"

"We have to end this before she gets hurt and mine finds out."

"So what? What if he finds out? She can't get hurt. It's not in her nature." Darius's head shifted, gently sliding his tongue over her inner lips. She inhaled sharply as he turned his head, lining his lips with hers, engaging in a deep kiss, as his tongue flickered in and out of the depths of her cave.

"Darius, baby, I can't take it."

He raised his head, smiling at her plea. He watched her intently for a moment.

"We don't have to play hide and seek."

"What? What are you talking about?" She hoped he would not say what she knew was about to come out of his mouth.

"I am here for you. We can do this. All you have to do is decide to be mine."

"Damn," she whispered to herself. This was why words were no good. How badly she longed to hear them, how good they would have felt in another situation. At another time. Now, they made her panic and feel slightly out of control.

Simone shook her head. "It's more complicated than that."

"Is it?" Opening his mouth wide, he extended his tongue and lightly licked her inner lips again, tugging them gently between his teeth. "Why...does...it...have...to...be?"

Lost at the pure thrill of excitement his tongue generated, Simone squealed in delight as her mind went blank. It actually did not seem that complicated at all.

CHAPTER 24

S he was far from stupid. Something was different. Darius normally did not give her much more than surface communication. She never really knew what he was thinking or feeling. He was so much different from the other athletes she dated. However, Tiffany had this game down to a science, convinced he was the one she could lasso into marriage.

She could tell when he was messing around. There were so many other players in this game. Many low-class skanks thought they could get a baller and live large. However, they could not compare to her. Her mother had taught her the game; she knew it inside out. She knew how to ignore the little side affairs and pay no attention to the possible one-night stands that overstepped their bounds and tried to claim her man.

This time, though, something was different. He was closing the door on their relationship and sealing her out of the equation. He had not said much, but that was normal. Yet, she could feel a difference in him and he was not falling for her normal stunts. She invited him out and he claimed he did not want to go. No problem, she offered to come over and pamper him instead. He barely responded, muttering something about not being up to it.

In her stilettos, garters, and lace bodice, she waited for him at his house. Wearing a small, red overcoat, she met him in the driveway, giving him her best seductress act. He was not happy to see her, but reluctantly let her inside. That much she could ignore. With ease, she slid out of the coat and watched his eyebrows raise as his lips parted. She knew she was on fire; she kept her body tight and perfect. What she had not been able to fix at the gym, liposuction took care of quite nicely. She teased him a little and danced for him, something he could never resist. However, midway through her performance, someone called his cell phone. He glanced at it, did a double take, and excused himself. He went in the other room to take the call. After staying in the other room for close to an hour, she was so pissed off. She considered leaving, but she was not that crazy. When he walked back into the great room, he seemed surprised to see her, as if he had forgotten she was there. He escorted her to the door, saying he had to get to an appointment. He had never denied her before and certainly never denied himself from having her.

She knew it was someone else. Someone he was keeping secret, but held dear. She invested too much into Darius Winfield to give up this easily. She decided to call him. Holding up her freshly manicured nails, Tiffany surveyed her hands. She would have to find a new manicurist; this one did an awful job and was not careful enough with the details. The call went straight to voicemail. She tried again, this time calling the house phone. The phone rang continuously until the voicemail picked up.

"Sorry I missed your call. Leave your message at the beep."

Tiffany sighed. The message was so plain, simple, and boring, just like Darius. It rather irked her that she was chasing him at all. Without his money and prestige, he would be lucky to get a look from her. Yet, life was what it was, and she did not mind biding her time to get what she was owed. Besides, after giving him a year of her life, he owed her a rock and access to those Benjamins.

"Hi, baby, it's me. Tiffany. I'm missing you, hoping we can get together later."

She placed the phone in its cradle and sat still for a few minutes. Then she picked it up again and dialed.

"Lindsey, it's me."

"Hey, girl. What's going on?" She could hear the reservation in Tiffany's voice. Lindsey had been her best friend since middle school and loved her unconditionally, but could not understand why she invested so much time in dating athletes. Lindsey believed in love and romance and all that other nonsense. However, she had proven that she had Tiffany's back no matter what and Tiffany knew Lindsey would not judge her.

"Something's wrong. Darius isn't traveling or anything, but I can't get him. I normally would do this myself, but he knows my car."

"I would think so since he bought it."

Tiffany laughed. "So, you mind taking me on a drive-by?"

"No problem. What are we trying to see?"

"I am trying to see where he is, or if he is home ignoring me."

"Uh-huh."

"Don't say it like that. What? You think I shouldn't check up on him, right?"

"Tiffany, you know how these athletes are. Why are you tripping?"

"I just have a feeling that's all."

"All right." Lindsey sighed. "Give me half an hour."

"Can't wait that long, damn!"

"Ten minutes." Lindsey laughed.

"Ten minutes." Tiffany placed the phone on the hook. She twirled her finger around the loose locks flowing from her crown, which looked perfect on her caramel complexion. That caliber of weave was worth every penny. She changed her eye color, opting for a lighter brown. She slipped into a snug Under Armour tank top, with matching low-rider pants and sneakers. Pulling back her hair, she tucked it into a bun at the base of her neck and pulled on an apple cap. Studying herself in the mirror, she shook her head. She had thought these reconnaissance missions were a thing of the past. Darius had been so easy until now. He was messing with a pro. He just did not know it.

CHAPTER 25

Simone could barely catch her breath. The orgasms rocked her to her very core, sending wave after magnetic wave through her. She went from hot to freezing cold to hot again. Darius watched her closely, intensely noting each change of her body, his hands still rubbing her until she seized them to hold them still. With every encounter, he documented how to take her to another level. She could not take any more. The multiple orgasms wiped her out, brought down her last barricade and, without realizing it, she was crying.

"What's wrong?" Darius had panic in his voice.

Simone tried to console him, smiling through the sobbing tears. "Nothing."

"Then why are you crying?"

"I honestly don't know."

"Did I hurt you?"

"No."

He pulled up behind her, spooning her and rubbing her stomach, with his elbow propped on the pillow to hold his head up. She could tell he had no clue what to say next. She was speechless, too. He held her and rubbed her while she shook with sobs that tore from her spirit. Finally, as her sobs subsided, and she sniffled, she looked for tissue to dry her face.

From the bedside accent table, he grabbed the box of Kleenex and handed it to her.

"Talk to me. Why are you crying?"

"I really don't know. I think it was part of the orgasm."

"Huh?"

"Yeah, if it's intense enough, it can make you lose control. I just felt a total release, and the tears came with it."

"Well, if that's what it was, then I am glad it happened."

He still sounded suspect.

Simone rolled over to face him. She licked the tip of his nose, and then gently bit his lip. "That's what happened."

"Has that ever happened before?"

"Once." That was all she could answer. She did not want to discuss Jackson with him, let alone think about him. She wanted to stay in the paradise Darius created every time they were together. They made love often, but during those quiet moments between, they shared their most intimate thoughts, beliefs, experiences, and dreams. She wanted to limit that type of interaction, to keep it to the sex so it would be easier to walk away. Yet, she could not seem to help herself.

"Once," he repeated in a slow whisper. He closed his eyes.

She wondered what he was thinking. She moved closer to him, wanting to inhale him, if she could. She had never felt so safe before, so completely protected. His arms were a fortress around her and she did not want to leave.

"I thought about you last week." His eyes were open, watching her again.

She smiled. "You did?"

"I wanted you with me. I wanted you to see Italy."

"I'm glad I was in your thoughts." She wondered if Miss Picture had gone with him. She wanted to ask who had gone with him, but knew better. She had no right to lay claim to him.

"I did. I kept thinking about you."

Simone smiled again, closing her eyes and feeling his heartbeat. Her fingers traced a light path up and down his torso. She was so in love with him, it hurt so good. There was nothing she could do with that wonderful feeling. Nothing. Except lay there and enjoy it while she could.

"I decided I wanted to do something for you."

"Really? You don't have to do anything for me."

"I know I don't have to, Simone. I said *I wanted to.*"

"Okay. So, what did you do?"

"Well, I bought you something, but you have to agree to take it before I give it to you. If you refuse, I will be upset."

She shook her head. "I can't take something from you, Darius. I know you. I know it's something wonderful that I can't really have because I can't have it wherever I am."

"See, you are making me upset already." His lips held a slight grin, but she knew he was serious.

"All right."

"So, no matter what, it's yours. Okay?"

"Okay."

He smiled. Like a child on Christmas morning, he reached under the bed. She closed her eyes and a huge smile graced her soft, angelic face. He had thought of her and bought her something. It was a nice gesture. As much as Jackson traveled, she could not remember the last time he thought of her and brought her something to show for it.

"Well, what do you think?"

Slowly opening her eyes, she gazed at the delicate golden bracelet as he held it up by the clasp with the Tiffany case in his other hand. She was speechless. It was magnificent. The gold seemed braided, lightly intertwined. From afar, it appeared to be a thin strand, but up close, she could tell the bracelet was, in fact, three or four silken cords of gold.

"Well, babe, what do you think?" He was anxious for a reaction.

"Oh my!" It was beautiful, and thin enough to be barely noticeable. She turned it over and saw the single word "mine" laced thinly on the backside of the bracelet. "It is so perfect, Darius. I...I don't know what to say."

"I saw it and I thought of you. Delicate. Beautiful. Feminine. Perfect."

"Damn." Back to speechless, she stared at him. How did he keep doing this to her? "What does 'mine' mean?"

"Mine."

"What?"

"It means mine."

"As in the bracelet is mine," she responded lightly, more to herself than to him.

"No, as in *you* are mine."

"Damn."

Most of her felt thrilled, but some tiny part in the back of her heart felt concerned. She was experiencing orgasm to the point of tears and now he was blatantly laying claim to her. This thing had already spun out of control.

CHAPTER 26

They finally left the master bedroom suite of the house. The intimacy of her gift, his outward label, and her realization made it necessary for her to do something normal to try to sort through her thoughts. She needed to cook a meal.

With Jackson out of town and Jasmine with her parents, Simone could give herself completely to Darius for another twenty-four hours. She worried how much deeper into this tunnel of doom they would dig during the next twenty-four hours. What worried her was not how far they would go, but her inability to stop it and her unwillingness to end it. It was as if she were watching a movie play out, helpless to do much more than watch. As she searched the stocked refrigerator for options, she felt his large hands cupping her backside.

"Stop." Simone giggled, moving forward a little as she glanced over her shoulder. She wore his T-shirt. She insisted he at least throw on a pair of shorts, hoping clothes would provide the blockage they needed.

"Do you ever touch yourself?" He pinned his lower torso to her backside.

Ignoring him, she pushed him back a little with her rear end as she bent over to open the vegetable bin.

"Simone?"

"Hmm." She was trying desperately to tune him out. She reached for the cucumbers and tomatoes. She glanced at the iceberg lettuce but chose the romaine instead. "Does she do your shopping?"

At the mentioning of "she," for a hot second, his playing stopped. "No."

"Who does?"

"How do you know I don't?"

Simone turned around with the selection of vegetables in her arm. "Please."

Darius smiled. "I've got a shopper."

"I bet you do."

"I wish you did."

"You wish I had a shopper? Or you wish I did your shopping?" At his smile, Simone sighed deeply. She placed the vegetables on the island. She had to address this, at least clarify her position. "Darius, why do you keep saying stuff like that? Why are you blurring the lines so much? We both have too much to lose." She turned back around to the refrigerator. She was in the mood for something simple. She pulled out the chicken breast thawing on the top shelf.

"I have nothing to lose."

The finality of his tone made her turn around, chicken breast in hand. Slightly, she turned her head and squinted. "I am married with a child."

"Simone, you can always leave."

For some strange reason, that stumped her. She knew she could leave. It was something she had considered. However, hearing it aloud, from the mouth of her lover, made it seem like a viable option.

Simone searched the cherry wood cabinets. "I could, but then I would have to answer to my daughter about it. Then what would I say?"

He was silent while she searched through the cabinets. Finally, she stumbled upon the seasonings.

"I haven't seen your daughter."

She looked up. He sounded so sincere. "You haven't?"

"No. You don't mention her much."

"Because of the nature of this thing, you know? It feels wrong."

"That's just it. I don't want anything about this to feel wrong. This is right."

Simone stopped moving for a moment and stared into his eyes. He still saw her through those puppy love lenses. When would he see her faults? When would his love fade?

"Will you feel like that six months from now? Or even six weeks from now? That's the thing, we *think* we are in love, but then everything is changed so easily. When you get tired of me or this. When the thrill passes. Then what? My daughter is constant and I am trying to keep her world stable and calm."

"I have felt like this for years, Simone." His voice was back to a whisper. "For years. Everything I dreamed we would be, we are and more. I didn't give my heart completely to anybody before; I always had this love for you just sitting there, blocking me. I pushed myself, tried to become the man I wanted to be, the man you could be proud of."

"I have always been proud of you. No matter what. You said you loved Miss Picture."

"I do. I love her like you love an annoying family member. I mean, I wish her the best. Would help her if she needed it, but us…we are not this."

Simone began slicing the chicken breasts into thin pieces, her eyes on him.

"Do you know what it feels like to have a crush that won't go away? A desperate sick feeling every time you see the person's face and know they probably don't even know or care you're alive. Do you know what that feels like over time?"

Simone stopped cutting. "I never made you feel like I didn't care."

"No, but life moved on, and I wasn't an option. I understood that. There was nothing I could do about it and about the feelings I have for you. I say I love you because I can't find another word, but it's deeper. It's more."

Simone kept cutting the chicken. She needed him to stop talking so she could piece out a sensible response, say something to lessen the deep tension in the kitchen. She had not thought about the levity of his crush, that this meant more to him than it did to her.

"Darius, I know—"

She was interrupted by a loud beep. She stared around the kitchen, wondering where the noise had come from. She had not started cooking yet. It could not be the smoke detector. At first, she did not notice Darius had moved easily to the far corner of the kitchen, the eating nook that contained the large table and chairs, and a low sofa the length of the back wall. Darius was fumbling with a wall panel. The loud beep repeated. This time, Simone went to Darius, noticing, for the first time, the pad contained an LCD screen. They watched a cream Infinity pull slowly past Darius's gate.

"Tiffany," he mumbled, shaking his head and crumbling.

"Who?"

"Tiffany." He gave her a slight grin and shrugged. "As usual, trust her to provide the entertainment. Watch this."

Simone finally realized it must be Miss Picture. The Infinity drove slowly past the gate.

"She is so stupid. She actually thinks I don't know she's here."

"My car!" Simone covered her mouth. "She is going to see my car!"

"No, I parked it behind my Hummer, in the second garage. She won't be able to see in there."

"What does she want?"

"Checking on me, I guess."

"Did you tell her or does she just suspect?"

Darius shrugged, a small smile playing on his lips. "I guess she suspects." He focused on the small screen. "Check this out. She is actually getting out."

Simone watched Darius, confused he found any humor in any of this. This woman could find out who she was and contact Jackson. She could be dangerous. Moreover, the fact that she suspected anything was troubling, which meant she and Darius were not as discreet as they had thought.

"Damn, this girl." Darius shook his head, chuckling as they watched the small figure peeking through the windows lining the front door. She disappeared from the screen and Darius moved quickly, pressing buttons until she was once again on the screen, picked up by another camera.

"Is this whole house wired?"

"Yep, I can see the entire thing."

Darius's cell phone rang softly. He shook his head, not bothering to check the phone. "Now she's calling, checking whether I am here. Ain't this a bitch?"

Next, the house phone rang. Darius's face held an incredulous expression as he leaned back onto the plush bench with folded arms, watching Miss Picture.

She walked to the garage and stood on her tiptoes, trying to see in. Then she walked around the entire house, peeking in windows. She assumed he was not home. They watched her scramble onto the deck in the back of the house and tiptoe to the sliding glass door. She pulled on it. Simone glanced at Darius.

"Don't worry, it's locked. I think."

Simone shook her head. *This chick is out of control*, she thought. It did not matter whether the door was locked or not. Miss Picture lifted the cushion on one of the seats.

"What is she doing?" Simone was not believing what was unfolding before her eyes. *This is one desperate chicken head.*

Transfixed, they both watched her unzip the cushion and withdraw a key.

"Motherfucker!" Darius stood up and walked out of the kitchen.

Simone did not know what to do. The chicken was already simmering in light olive oil. She could not just run out of the kitchen and burn down the entire house. She was not scared of this little girl; she could handle her. However, she surely did not want a witness to her indiscretion. She did not want to be in the position of being caught.

Darius's head reappeared through the wide door. "Don't worry. Stay in here. I will get rid of her."

Then he disappeared.

CHAPTER 27

India had left out so many details. T. Lynn Taylor was the truth. There was no doubting it. Her office was larger than the managing partner's office of his firm, and she sat before him simple but elegant. He expected a hardcore woman-hating man. Instead, she was feminine and alluring, clear-eyed and polite. Her voice was sexy even though it was professional. He suddenly felt nervous; he did not want to disappoint this woman. He wanted to seem like a brother with something.

"India thinks highly of you."

"I doubt that." Jackson shifted his tie and glanced around the immaculate office.

"She does. I wouldn't exaggerate." She leaned forward, resting her arms on her desk. "You are more attractive than I thought you'd be."

Jackson looked up and met her eyes.

She smiled. "Forgive me for being so forward. I hope I didn't make you uncomfortable."

"No. You didn't."

"So, the first time we meet is right before the hearing, huh?" She turned gently in the swivel chair, reaching for a thick file on the edge of the white oak antique desk. "I am sorry for the delay."

"Not a problem." Jackson's eyes were on the file. "We have both been on travel, so meeting before this was impossible."

"I received information from your investigator. Martia?"

He nodded.

"I think we can find a solution at this phase. I can't see this thing going much further." She stood, and he watched her hair bounce as she moved.

What a fantastic creature, he thought. What was wrong with him? He was going to a sexual harassment hearing on a Sunday afternoon, and there he was, thinking about screwing his attorney.

He shook his head. "How? How can we settle it?"

"Well, according to the information provided by Martia, Ms. Nina has been fired from several positions over the past three years and has alleged sexual harassment in all of them. So, we have records, all the pleadings in the cases before they were either settled or dismissed. There is a huge credibility problem here."

Jackson nodded, feeling the lump in his throat dissipating. "Lynn, I just need this thing to go away."

She eyed his wedding band. "I bet you do."

"I can't lose my career over—"

Lynn shook her head and her mane bounced. "Jackson," she purred, the tips of her fingers pressed together. "You aren't listening."

Jackson stopped talking, nodding to signal his deference.

"I have already spoken to her attorney. Let him know just how I am planning to play this thing. The information I already have on her, things he didn't know. He began to see things my way. Trust me. His client will have a different approach at this meeting."

"What about the firm's counsel?"

"Spoke with him as well. Informed him that we will consider not suing the firm if they facilitate mediating this thing."

"Suing the firm? Damn, you said that?"

"Jackson, my dear." She made a clicking noise with her mouth, turning in the swivel chair, her hair bouncing again. "They were in the process of selling you down the river and settling this thing."

"Damn it! India was right."

"Of course, she was. I taught her well."

Jackson watched Lynn talk, watched the way her lips moved as she accentuated her words. What else had she taught India?

"So, let's go get this thing settled." She stood, revealing toned legs in a short skirt. Her suit jacket was fitted and tapered at the waist, giving him a full view of her round bottom. She tugged at the bottom of her jacket, lifted her briefcase, and eyed Jackson coyly. He wanted to grip her ass with both his hands. *Pull it together. She represents me. I am in enough trouble.*

"You ready?" She smiled.

Jackson realized he had not stood up. He was caught and her smile said it all.

"Yes." Jackson stood up quickly. He felt nervous. He did not want to see Nina or face the firm's representation. He did not want to answer aloud for his behavior. He had risked everything for a piece of ass. Ass that was not even that good. He was embarrassed to have Lynn see Nina, to witness how low he had been willing to stoop for a nut. However, it was too late now and there was no looking back. He shifted his eyes, trying to gain his composure.

"Jackson, look at me."

He glanced up. Lynn was no longer smiling, no longer looking flirty. In that instant, she turned into a no-nonsense, could-slit-your-throat-without-blinking type of woman.

"Jackson, it's game time. It's time for your game face."

He nodded. She opened the door to her office and, placing her hand on his back, escorted him through it.

CHAPTER 28

"What the fuck?"

Tiffany turned on her heels, surprise slamming her against the couch. She stumbled a bit before she pulled herself together. *What the hell is he doing here?* she thought, as deep heat flooded her as she became aware that she could not explain standing in his large family room, peering through the open day planner on the desk.

"I didn't know you were home."

"Obviously." Darius stared at her; arms folded across his well-defined muscular chest.

She looked him up and down, noticing the loose shorts hanging low enough to see his hairs. He smelled like sex. Like another woman's sex. How dare he be so bold as to confront her, smelling like another woman? Had he lost his mind?

"How the fuck did you get into my house?"

"Who are you talking to like that?" Tiffany knew she was dead-ass wrong, but her anger overruled her rationality. She should not have had to have a hidden key. He should have given one to her by now. "Who do you think you are, talking to me like that?"

"Don't walk into my house talking shit. You got some fucking nerve. How the fuck did you get a spare key?"

Tiffany was recalling everything she had surveyed so far. Why did he smell like sex? There was a Ford in the garage, behind the Hummer. She never saw it before. "You gotta woman up in here?"

"Tiffany. This is my house. You got that. Mine. You just played yourself. Go."

"Who the fuck are you talking to? You got a bitch up in here and now you are kicking me out?"

His head tilted as he dropped his hands to his sides. "*Get the fuck out of my house!*" Darius roared, his voice ripping the air, tearing through the house like a monsoon. She had never heard him yell and had never seen him enraged before. He had never spoken to her like that before. She had to resort to weakness to counter his anger. Tears always worked on soft ones like Darius.

"Is she here?" Tiffany whispered, her expert tear running down her cheek. "Are you in here with another woman?"

Her tears startled him. He looked as uneasy as she felt while he was screaming. He stared at her for a second, squinting.

"Darius, how could you do this to us?"

"Bitch, do you think this is *The Young and the Restless*? You don't know me. Don't game me. Get the fuck outta here. Your ass better not whip out any more keys I don't know about. In fact, I will have the locks changed. You just played yourself."

She had played the entire thing wrong. She knew it. There was no way to cover that she had broken into his house and was preparing to go through his things. How had she been so careless? Fuck him. He was not worth this much hassle. She could land another baller. However, it bothered her that the bitch was in the house, listening to him yelling at her. She could not stand the thought of another woman having won.

"No, you played yourself." Tiffany squared her shoulders. The tears and hurt demeanor disappeared as quickly as it had come. "Fuck you and fuck your trifling bitch!"

"This is the last time I am telling you to leave!" Darius's voice sounded like a low rumble approaching thunder.

She could smell food coming from the kitchen. *That heffa is in the kitchen cooking?* "Tell your girlfriend I peeped her little raggedy-ass Ford Explorer, and I got her plate. I can figure out who she is. Tell her she shouldn't have messed with what's mine."

Tiffany shouted the words over her shoulder as she sauntered toward the back door. She thought about putting on a show and walking out the front door instead, just to enrage Darius more. That would allow her to walk through the entire house and try to get a glimpse of the woman. What could Darius do to stop her? However, as soon as the words left her lips, she felt Darius snatch her by the arm, spinning her around to face him. Holding her arms tightly, he pinned her against the sliding glass door.

Through clenched teeth and barely above a whisper, Darius warned, "Don't you ever threaten me. Don't play with me. I am not to be fucked with."

Searing pain surged through her arms, but she was too frightened to do anything. She had never seen Darius like this. He always seemed so easygoing and laid-back, so predictable. She never knew he had this side to him and it frightened and excited her.

"Darius, please put me down."

"Do you hear me?" He shook her slightly, his grip tightening, and his lip curled. She felt sure both her arms were going to be broken by the time he released his grip. "Do not threaten her."

Tiffany opened her mouth and then quickly clamped it shut. She nodded frantically, real tears falling down her face. He stared at her for a few seconds, as if deciding whether he should release her or do her some other harm. Then he let go, relaxing into his normal stance. He seemed like his regular self again, with no trace of the anger he demonstrated seconds before.

The sudden change terrified her. She ran through the sliding door, jumped off the deck, and back to the waiting car.

Opening the door to the cream-colored Infinity, Tiffany hopped in the seat as she panted. Her arms crisscrossed, her hands rubbing the painful spots he had gripped.

"What's up? Did you find anything?"

"Hell yeah! I found a six-foot-two, two-hundred-thirty-pound pissed off fucker wondering why I had broken into his house."

"Oh, shit!" Lindsey put her foot on the gas and sped off the property. "What did he say?"

"At first, he was normal, arguing. Then he told me I had to leave. His bitch was still there. Then, I said something about the woman and finding out who she is, and he freaked out."

"What? Did he lay hands on you?"

"No, he pinned me against the wall and screamed. That is not like him."

"Yeah, but you got caught breaking and entering. I mean, what did you expect?"

"Yeah, but he didn't freak out until I mentioned that bitch." Tiffany sighed, leaning back in the seat, trying to fight back tears. She did not have Darius like she thought and her game was not as tight as she thought. She allowed Darius to get a sniff of something else and the hoe had won. That was her fault.

"Shit, am I that easily replaced?"

"Girl, please!" Lindsey seemed uneasy. "Just leave it alone."

"I'ma leave it alone. For now, anyway."

CHAPTER 29

Listening to every insult hurled out of Miss Picture's potty mouth, she considered going in the other room and confronting her. Only for a second, though. She had not had to fight since middle school and she was not about to start now. Besides, in her opinion, anyone desperate to sneak around someone's property was trifling and thirsty. That she had hidden a spare key was ridiculous.

Simone wondered why things had become so quiet after Miss Picture yelled that she could find out who she was. She must have left after saying that. Simone flipped the chicken curry and stirred the buttered rice. Part of her wondered if Miss Picture would make good on her threat. Would she look her up? Would she find Jackson and reveal Simone's secret? Of course, she would if she could. What scorned woman would not?

Simone's hand trembled, but she refused to acknowledge it. She would stay calm, determined not to be easily shaken by this simple-ass woman and her foolish act. She spooned rice onto two plates and scooped the curry chicken with vegetables on top of the mounds. She chose the small table in the corner and set the two plates on it. After pouring a glass of white wine, she sat on the bench and waited for Darius. She had seen the car speed out of the yard on the small screen, but he had not returned.

Ten minutes later, Simone started to worry. Miss Picture must have put doubt in his mind. Where was he? She stood up and surveyed the mammoth-sized kitchen. She did not want to eat without him. Simone tiptoed to the kitchen door. What if Miss Picture did not leave with the car and she and Darius were in the other room making love? What if she walked in on them? Would she be able to stop herself from feeling hurt, rejected, and betrayed? She slowly pushed the swinging door.

"Darius?"

"Yeah, babe."

"What's wrong?"

"Nothing. I was just waiting for you."

"I was waiting for you, too." Simone glanced around the room. "She left?"

Darius bobbed his head as if he were nodding it to some hip-hop beat. "Yup."

"That was interesting."

"Not for me."

She noticed his bloodshot eyes. "What's wrong?"

Darius remained silent as he leaned forward with his head hung low.

"Darius?"

Simone moved slowly toward him, fear knotting her insides. He had to choose, and he was choosing his girlfriend. Well, of course, he would. She still chose her husband.

"Simone, I want you. I want this. I want more."

Feeling an acute sense of loss, Simone was quiet. She heard the plain and simple words.

"I am putting an end to my other life. My life before you. I want it to be worth something."

"I am giving you all I can give." Simone's voice was fragile and shaking, mixed with tears streaming down her face.

"No. That's not true." He wrapped his arm around her thighs and pulled her into him, burying his face between her thighs, inhaling deeply. He loved the way she smelled. "You can give me all of you, if you wanted to."

"I can't—"

"You could, Simone, if you wanted to."

Simone rubbed the back of Darius's head. "Come eat." She took his hands in hers. He did not look up. "Darius, come on, baby. Come and eat."

"Simone. Simone..." he trailed off, his voice now cracking.

Simone leaned down and kissed the top of his smooth bald head. His hands caressed the small of her back and then fondled her bare bottom. Parting her thighs, he gently stroked her center, as her arms wrapped loosely around his head. Stroking her until she purred, he lifted her T-shirt, circled her belly button with his tongue, and lightly licked it. He grabbed her bottom again and his touch was less gentle and firmer. Swiftly, he spun her around and pulled her down on his lap, positioning her on his erection.

"I want you, Simone. I need you, babe. Give Daddy some. Please."

The more he talked, the wetter Simone became.

"Are you getting it wet for me?"

Simone moaned her response, her mouth opened, her head thrown back. She could feel his manhood growing. He lightly bit her back as he reached around and stroked under her hood. Simone released a sharp gasp as she buckled, her legs stretching out before her, shaking frantically, as waves of intense pleasure washed over her.

"Let it go, baby."

"Oh, God," she cried out between euphoric waves. "Darius, baby…" She shook uncontrollably, exploding with a feeling she had never felt from any man. Not even Jackson.

Darius slightly raised her hips, slid his hand between her bottom and his abdomen, and released his throbbing steel. Rising, she lowered herself on him, enveloping him inside her fleshy folds.

As the T-shirt bunched up around her neck, she struggled to pull it off as he stroked her with deep thrusts, as she moved up and down, bucking, riding her buck.

As his thrust became quicker and deeper, he said it repeatedly, a little louder each time in her ear, "Mine. Mine. Mine."

Pushing with all his might, she smiled slightly. She did not want to. She could not help it. It was her natural response, her instinct, the primal her that did not heed societal expectations, and what was supposed to be right.

"Yours," she whispered with each thrust, matching his intimate chant. The louder she said it, the more intense his thrust became until he bucked, releasing a wild shake with her feet planted firmly on the floor. They both slid to the floor as Simone's second climax kicked in.

"Yes, baby, damn," mumbled Darius, his hands touching her liquid love.

"Yours, Darius. I'm all yours," Simone confirmed, before drifting off into a sex-induced slumber.

CHAPTER 30

N ina sat straight; her short haircut neatly tapered around the back of her neck. Jackson had to fight the urge to smack the back of her head. The sight of her pissed him off more than he could have imagined. Putting on his game face had been difficult. He grew weak in the knees at the thought of spreading his life out before a judge. However, seeing her changed everything. He felt glad he had fired her; glad she was out of his life. He looked forward to crushing her and embarrassing her in front of these White boys.

India was right. Lynn was worth her weight in gold. As they entered the neat conference room, Lynn walked right past Nina, never bothering to acknowledge her. He watched Nina observing Lynn's fitted suit and bountiful bouncing hair, as the White boys jumped out of their seats to shake her hand and make small talk. They wanted her, too. She was gorgeous and her beauty crossed color lines. She knew how to small talk with them, too. Instead of talking about the case, she sat in a chair, teasing Nina's attorney about the latest developments in college sports. The law firm's attorney seemed riveted by Lynn, displaying more personality while small talking with her than in any previous meeting Jackson had seen him.

He looked at Nina with a fire burning in his eyes. He had never wanted to hit a woman before now. He expected her to smirk or at least look triumphant. However, Lynn had sucked all the woman's glory out of the air and Nina paled in comparison, eyeing her enviously.

When the judge arrived, they all resumed professional decorum. Lynn whipped out a pair of serious eyeglasses, which Jackson felt were more for appearances than need. For the first time, she slowly appraised Nina. She held Nina's gaze until Nina looked away. Then, for added effect, Lynn leaned over and whispered in Jackson's ear.

"Nod your head like I am saying something. This is going to be easier than I thought."

Jackson nodded affirmatively, his eyes on Nina, who watched with a look of frustration. She hated Lynn. That much was already evident and Lynn would use it to her advantage.

The judge was actually in retirement, serving as a mediator. Lynn had moved this thing from a formal setting to a quasi-mediation outside of the courthouse. After the introductions, the judge glared coldly at Jackson. He imagined he knew what he was thinking, sure he thought this Black man was capable of sexual harassment.

The judge asked several questions, involving whether Nina's counsel had explained to her that a deal had been reached. Apparently not, because she fussed, pouted, and raised her voice. Meanwhile, Lynn sat with a thin manila envelope on the table, tapping it lightly. While Nina's attorney nodded, she adamantly shook her head, forcing the judge to order a brief recess while counsel reached one accord with his client.

They took a brief recess while she and her attorney discussed the case in the hall. Jackson sat watching them, not bothering to look away when Nina glared his way. Jackson watched in amazement as the same manila folder Lynn had tapped on the table was now being held by the opposing attorney and he thumbed through it, pointing out information to Nina. With each point, she seemed weaker, as if he were jabbing her with a fork. When they returned, the look of utter defeat on her face made Jackson's heart skip a beat. This thing was over. Or, as Simone would say, "The fat lady has sung."

"Let's get something to eat."

"Where do you want to eat?"

"I am tired." Lynn sighed. "Let's go to my place. I will order carryout."

Jackson felt startled by her response, but he was not going to argue. He agreed, reveling in the happiness of being done with the case. He wanted to share his good news with the love of his life, but he had never told Simone about the case in the first place. Still, he wanted to hear her voice.

While Lynn went to the restroom, Jackson called Simone's cell phone. Straight to voicemail. He sighed, not wanting to think about his dirt and all the things she had to tolerate. Today reflected his mindset and the confusion he caused. He had not been faithful, but he always figured he could easily manage Simone. However, Nina had shaken his entire existence. She dredged up his behavior and put it out in public, schooling his coworkers and colleagues. He was feeling uncomfortable at work, knowing his colleagues knew. He could only blame himself.

Now he was thinking about Lynn's bouncing hair, wondering what she possibly saw in him. Maybe he was reading too much into it. Maybe she really wanted to eat. Lynn strolled out of the bathroom, her head tilted to the side, her briefcase bouncing against her leg. He wondered how old she was. Maybe five years older than him. Men turned and looked as she passed. She seemed to not notice. She was staring at him. Unblinking. Thinking. Strategizing. He wanted to know what was on her mind.

"Ready?" She walked past him.

He fell in step with her stride. "Ready for what, exactly?"

"For me."

Damn. I don't want to do this, he thought, as he chuckled. "I actually don't know."

"Really," she paused, but kept walking slowly. "I'm interested. I'm interested in you."

"I'm married."

"I'm committed."

Committed. Interesting choice of words. He still wondered about her and India, why India seemed so intimately knowledgeable about Lynn.

"Ride with me."

He shrugged, opening the driver's door to her Mercedes. As she slid into the seat, her skirt hiked up and he glanced down at her supple thigh. He shut the door carefully. He lied to avoid telling Simone about the hearing. He said he was out of town this weekend. Therefore, technically, he had the night free until he had to return home tomorrow. Besides, Simone was not taking his calls anyway, probably still having a temper tantrum about his comment the other night. How could he turn down the opportunity to taste such a fine, exquisite creature as Lynn? No man could turn her down unless he was a damn fool.

It felt a little awkward since he had not seen this option coming. She navigated between flirting and professional very easily, but he had not gotten the vibe she wanted him until the offering. Shoot, who in the hell was he to refuse?

She drove like a bat out of hell. She never looked at him. They did not speak. She drove with her eyes locked on the road. She turned on the music. He sat quietly, watching her, wondering when she was going to remember he was there. The jazz tunes filled the car. He leaned back in the seat, exhaling slowly and loudly. It was over. The entire thing with Nina was over and the stress of it was slowly peeling away from him.

At a red light, Lynn slid out of her tight suit jacket. The blouse underneath hugged her torso perfectly, laying across her flat stomach and clinging to her full bosom. She hummed to the music, swaying her head and snapping her fingers. The stress of the day, the stress that Lynn seemed to have been completely unaffected by, was peeling from her as well. Her bouncing and behaving hair shook and swayed in tune to the music.

She lived in Mitchellville. He assumed she was a Virginia-type of chick, with all her knowledge about the University of Virginia and easy hobnobbing with the White boys. However, she seemed to fit in this environment, as an easier smile formed on her face as she zoomed past equivalent Benzes and other Black professionals stripping away the day. The Mercedes SL turned into an upscale community of single-family homes.

"My home is new, less than a year old."

Jackson nodded. He lived five minutes from there. Did she not know he also lived in Mitchellville? *Shit. I am shitting where I sleep. This is pushing my good luck too far.* However, he dismissed his concerns, which was typical of a whore. He would not bump into Simone since they were already at her house. She pulled down the long driveway and into the garage. They sat in silence as the garage door lowered behind them.

"Welcome to *mi casa*."

CHAPTER 31

S he kicked off her heels in the car. Picking them up, she climbed out of the car, leaving everything else. Jackson followed, looking around the spacious, three-car garage. "You live here by yourself?"

She smiled at him and walked up the few steps leading to the rear entry. Once again, and like a trained dog, he followed the bitch in heat. As he stepped through the door, he purposely clamped his mouth shut to keep it from falling open. The house was humongous. Easily, it was triple the size of his house. It was beautiful. Decorated in autumn colors, the deep reds and subtle golds instantly soothed his nerves, as did the music pouring through the house.

She hit a small panel on the wall that looked like a mini iPod and tossed her shoes into the corner. She took a few steps forward, her skin shining in the dim, evening light. Unbuttoning her blouse, she stared at Jackson, and her camisole was completely exposed.

She leaned into his chest. "So, why someone like her, huh?"

For a second, he did not realize whom she meant.

"Nina. Why?"

He shrugged. "I don't know. Easy, I guess."

"Easy?"

They both laughed. Lynn handed him a glass and reached for another. He stood close behind her, staring at her perfect ass. She turned around and chuckled, placing the glass on the counter.

"Wine?"

Jackson shook his head. He needed more than that. "Something stronger. After this day, I need something stronger."

"Ah, I've got something for you."

She swayed over to the cabinet and removed a cookbook. Between the pages was a small brown packet, which she waved in front of him. "I got the ganja, man."

"Aww, shit!" Jackson shook his head. He had not puffed since undergrad.

He sat next to her as she sipped the wine and rolled two joints. Standing, she seductively looked down at Jackson and moved into the kitchen, where she turned on the eye of the stove to light the joint. Then, closing her eyes and taking a deep pull, she returned to him, bent down, and blew the smoke in his face. He watched her thick hair as she stood back. The cloud of smoke instantly relaxed him.

As she passed him the joint, she grabbed him by the hand and led him to her huge family room. Jackson pulled on the joint and held the smoke deeply in his chest, feeling the ganja coil around his lungs, before slowly exhaling. They both fell back on the couch, laughing and passing the joint between them. It was easier to breathe now, to think about Simone without slamming into a brick wall of guilt. Yet, the soul-stirring crooning of Will Downing soothed his soul, helping him to forget about his wife.

Standing before him, with her arms stretched high above her head, her hands rhythmically moving about like a snake charmer, with precision, Lynn gyrated and moved with the ease of a professional stripper. Winding her hips down to the floor, she crossed her arms around her and easily pulled the silk blouse up over her head. After twirling the blouse over her head, she flung it across the room. Peering into his eyes, she unzipped her skirt and allowed it to fall around her fuchsia-painted toes, and danced slowly, but seductively swaying, as she stepped out of the skirt. Moving close to him, she leaned down, resting her palms on his thighs. Jackson was enjoying every move of her seductive dance as he pressed the tip of the joint between her glossy lips. She drew long and hard, his eyes glued to her breast protruding from the bra, as she pressed her mouth against his, releasing the smoke.

He could no longer resist her. The urge to dig deep into her overwhelmed him. Sensuously, he stroked her cleavage. "Come here," he whispered.

He kissed her lips lightly. He wanted to run his hands through that hair. She laughed and straddled his lap, still swaying to the music, still rocking her hips. Her pressure against his tip thrilled him. She bit his lip. He moaned. She bit a little too hard.

"I am curious, you know?" she admitted.

"Yeah. I figured."

"Let me see."

"What do you want to see?"

Her hands slid between her thighs, groping his hardness as it pressed against her inner thigh. "Let me see."

He smiled, listening to the zipper unzipping and sighing as her hand masterfully stroked him.

"Ohhhhhh. No wonder she was grittin' on me."

Jackson laughed. "Nina would've acted that way no matter what. You're fucking beautiful."

"Hmm..." For a second, Lynn seemed clear-headed. She stared at him with a look of sincerity breaking through the shadow of her façade. "Thank you."

She kissed him, her tongue filling his mouth. Wrapping his arms around her, he kissed her passionately as if she were his woman. He sucked her tongue. He felt her lift slightly and then her pressure overwhelmed him as she slid down on top of his shaft. She was so wet he did not have time to prepare himself. In an instant, he was completely devoured by her inner sweetness.

Lynn lifted her hips slowly and Jackson stared at her hair as it swayed to the rhythm of this sexy lawyer blowing his mind. Suddenly she stood, turning around and straddling him again, with her back to him. Opening his eyes, Jackson leaned forward and buried his face in her thick mane and inhaled deeply. Her hair smelled like freesia, for a hot minute reminding him of Simone. Quickly, he dismissed his wife from his thoughts. At least until he squirted his jism.

"You are on fire," he moaned, as she slid up and down the length of him. "Damn, woman, you've got some good pussy."

He wrapped his hand in her hair, gripping it as she went up and down. Then he slid both hands to her breasts, holding and rubbing them from behind as her motion went faster and she panted louder. Her vagina tightened, clenching him until he wanted to scream, her friction felt like a fitted glove. Refusing to explode before she creamed, he stood up and wrapped his arms around her waist to keep her from falling.

She released her lock on him, sliding down and turning around to lick him gently. It was rare for a woman to lick him after he had been inside of her. Most did not seem to want to taste their own juices. However, she seemed to enjoy how she tasted as she carefully licked every inch of him and groaning in the process. Her hand was between her thighs, which were spread wide. He stepped back and watched her, with her chin and shoulders resting on the floor, her ass tooted up in the air, her hand furiously rubbing her button. He entered from behind, pushing and stroking faster and slower, trying to feel every inch of her.

"Stop. Be still," she whispered.

He stopped moving and watched her stroke herself, her torso and hips moving methodically as if riding a tidal wave. She reminded him of the dolphin dance he used to do when he was a kid, but every time she rose, her velvet would push back onto his girth. With each stroke, she groaned and pushed herself onto him, causing him to groan. She repeated it until she finally yelled out. He gripped her hips, keeping himself inside her through the orgasm, feeling her vagina spasm. Then he exploded.

For a few seconds, they absorbed each other's presence in silence, while Jackson tried to compose himself. He wanted some more. He stuck his fingers deep into her vagina. He could not believe how tight she felt. Lynn groaned, her hips instantly moving with his hand. *She is truly a freak. My kind of woman.* She was ready for more.

Then a fake cough filled the air. They both looked up to see India standing in the kitchen, her bag on the floor, her mouth wide open. Jackson scrambled to find his pants. However, Lynn simply smiled as she continued to rub her pussy as she watched India.

CHAPTER 32

India slow-walked from the kitchen into the large family room. He yanked up his pants, watching Lynn stroke herself with one hand and twirl her hair with the index finger of her other hand.

"Jackson… What the fuck?"

"What…what are you doing here?" he stammered.

"I live here."

He glanced at Lynn. Her eyes were fixated on India. Just like that, the chameleon attorney had changed again, shifted in her stance. Although she still looked like a seductress, she seemed desperate for India to see her and say something. She wanted a reaction from India, was hoping for some drama. He understood immediately he had been played, used to strike some vendetta against India.

"I told you," Lynn whispered, a tear rolling down her cheek. "I told you what he was."

India still did not look at her, refusing to acknowledge her. India stared at Jackson with pure energy that terrified him.

"Jackson, why are you here?"

"I guess I don't really know." He looked at Lynn. "Why am I here, Lynn?"

India removed her small frame eyeglasses and ran her hand through her hair. Propping her hands on her waist, she turned around and surveyed the large room.

"So, you came to my living space and fucked all over it."

"I didn't know it was your space. I didn't know you lived here. Lynn said it was her home."

India did not blink, staring at Jackson with squinted eyes. The truth was forcing its way through her and she seemed to be fighting it. "It is."

"So, you are roommates?" Jackson asked the rhetorical question with a smirk.

"I told you," whispered Lynn. "You said his name in your sleep. Wanted me to take his case. Talk about him all the time. I could see it."

India looked at Jackson and shook her head. "How much?"

"Huh?" Jackson felt heat invading his body. He was embarrassed and disgusted. India's expression was a mirror to his actions and indiscretions. This was not something he could hide. There were no more secrets for him. Here was someone who knew his dirt and guided him to redemption, only to find him naked in her house fucking. Incorrigible. What else could she think, but that he was incorrigible? He was. A married hoe. Slut puppy. Tramp. Skeezer. A nasty, low-life motherfucker.

"How much has she had?"

He shrugged his shoulders, aware he seemed like a bigger idiot by just the one move.

"Where have you been?" Lynn muttered.

India looked at her for the first time. Peeling her eyes away from Jackson had taken some effort. He could feel the pull.

"You're back to dick, just like that, huh? You were with him, weren't you?" Lynn accused.

India remained silent. She walked over to her, reached down, and pulled her up from the floor. She did not seem to mind that she was butt naked, smelling of drugs and sex.

"You have to stop this," India muttered.

"No!" Lynn pushed away from her, the thick hair swaying.

Jackson watched her hips as she stood up and then looked at the floor. He was so fucked. How could he still be thinking about sex?

"Get off of me! Answer the fucking question! Where were you?"

"What does it matter? You're here, fucking my boss."

"Answer me!"

"Yes," India answered her, their eyes locked. "You know who I am. You know what this is. How many times do we have to do this?"

"You're killing me." Lynn tapped her chest, her fingers tapping against the top of her heaving breasts. "You're killing me, India, and you don't even fucking care!"

"I love you." The words left India's mouth with such force that they seemed to slam into Lynn as she stumbled back. "I love you! Why isn't that enough? Damn, Lynn, what do you want me to do? I am here. I am not leaving. I can't question you. I can't say shit. Yes, I was with Ray. I fucked him. It meant nothing, but a fuck. You know that. This…this hurts me."

Lynn watched her as silent tears poured from her face, gently wetting her breasts.

Jackson felt uncomfortable. He did not understand what type of relationship thing they had going on, what the arrangement was, but Lynn's pain felt so palpable that he felt like an intruder for watching.

India walked toward her, their eyes never separating. They stood with foreheads pressed together, India muttering words of love and Lynn nodding. The seductive queen that had ruled the boardroom and Jackson for the last few hours had turned into a passive lover. India was the queen. She wrapped her arms around Lynn, holding her closer, continuing to talk.

Jackson looked around for his clothes. He needed to get the hell out of Dodge.

"Let me take you to your room," India whispered to Lynn. They moved slowly down the wide hallway. India looked over her shoulder and mouthed the word *stay*.

Jackson did not dare leave.

"I'm not gay and my sexuality isn't at issue here. What is at issue is why you can't keep your dick in your pants."

"Ha. Talk about a hypocrite." Jackson leaned his head toward the opened window, hoping the air would clear his head. "So, what, you're a DL sister? That's a new one."

"No. I fell in love with a woman. Once. I am not gay. I don't want any other woman. I love men. So, I am just in No-Man's Land." She grimaced. "Bad use of words."

"Yo, whatever. Your ass is bisexual then. At least say that."

"I don't have to define my shit. I ain't got kids to answer to. I ain't taking care of nobody else. What's your excuse?"

She shifted the old BMW sharply, causing Jackson to lurch forward.

"I don't have one."

"Shit, at least you know you're pathetic."

"Yeah. I know."

They rode in silence for a few minutes until India broke the silence. "So, I know you won since you were having a celebratory fuck."

"Come on, India, leave it alone already."

"No. I am mad as hell. I love her. You had no right violating her."

"You told her you were fucking someone else."

"Did you tell your wife about the mediation?"

That shut him up.

"Damn. You are a piece of shit."

Jackson did not look at her. He did not respond. What the hell could he say? He was relying on a sexually confused female for advice, who saw his confusion. He snorted.

"Where did you park?"

Jackson pointed toward the office building across the street from the courthouse. "I parked two blocks away."

"Why didn't you park in the garage?"

Jackson shrugged. "The mediation wasn't in the courthouse. It was in another building. Besides, the garage is closed on Sundays."

"Goddamn. I am tired as hell. I am driving around DC looking for your car, after finding you fucking my significant other."

Jackson stared straight ahead. Where was his damn car? He stared up and down the empty street.

"You obviously got towed. *Shit!*" India screamed. "I drove into DC for nothing."

"How about shit I am so busted? How am I out of town and returning without my ride? How am I going to get my joint out of tow without Simone finding out?"

"No longer my problem. You violated mine."

"Just take me home." Stinking and filthy, smelling like another woman and drugs, he would go home and let Simone see the real him. The flawed him. He might as well man up and tell her what he had been through, about the mediation and his decisions immediately thereafter. He needed some type of help, some saving grace. Simone had been that for him before. Maybe she would again, but even if she was not, she deserved to know the truth about him. Tears filled his eyes. The drug was affecting him, he knew. It did not matter, though. He was going to come clean and tell Simone everything, even if it cost him their life together. She deserved to know and if she chose to leave, he would not fight her.

CHAPTER 33

Simone looked at the clock. She had to come straight to work from Darius's house. They completely lost track of time, him rubbing her with oils in the wee hours of the morning. However, she had peeled herself away and made it to work.

"Where have you been?" Celeste asked.

"Huh? You called here before eight?"

"No, heifer. I've been calling you all weekend and all day yesterday. Where have you been?"

"Nowhere. I just took some downtime. Turned off the ringers."

"Well, I came by. House was empty as a ghost town. I knew Jackson was out of town. I figured we could meet and hang out."

"I'm sorry I missed you. I wish I had caught up with you, though. We haven't had a girl's day out in the longest time."

"Didn't you hear my voice messages? I left about a hundred of them. Tell you the truth, if you hadn't answered your work phone this morning, I was going to call the police."

"Aw, Celeste, I am fine."

"Well, anyway, what's been going on?"

"Absolutely nothing," Simone lied. So much was going on. She fell in love. She experienced the best loving ever. Her husband no longer had a stranglehold on her heart. She was a terrible person. She had phone sex with Tim…twice. She felt relief whenever she thought about her newfound freedom. She was happy again. Yet, she could not admit any of that to Celeste. She simply would not understand.

"David has been tripping lately."

"Why?"

"I don't know. It's nothing he said, but I can just feel it."

"What?" Simone glanced at the clock. She wondered whether Darius had opened his eyes yet, whether he was awake and aware she was gone. "What can you feel?" Simone imagined Darius's fingertips on her lips, his thick fingers in her mouth.

"Since I got home from the hospital, it's like he's angry at me, but not really."

"Girl, you know he goes through this every time. He has to adjust to how scary the thought of losing you is."

"Yeah. Kind of. He never seemed mad at me before. Now everything I do and say irritates him. Every time I leave, he just stares at me."

"Yeah, because he wants you to stay your wild ass home." They both laughed, Simone giggling softly into the phone. "You know I am telling the truth. You run the streets too damn much."

"No, I don't. Not any more than anyone else."

"You're not just anyone else, Celeste. You know that."

"See, that's what I mean. It's so easy for everyone to tell me not to do anything, to sit still, and be very careful. I have done that before and guess what?"

"You still got sick."

"I still got sick, damn it. So, I am damned if I do, damned if I don't!"

"Celeste that's what David thinks. He wants you to slow down. You didn't have to drive down to the class reunion two days after being discharged. You know he was probably scared as hell."

"I wanted to—"

"That's what marriage is, right? Not about what you want, but about making y'all work. So, if David needs you to slow down to feel better, then—" Simone heard the sharp intake of air and then the slow exhale. "Celeste."

"I'm here. I have to think. What are you doing later? Want to grab dinner?"

Simone rolled her eyes and stared at her computer screen, ignoring her friend for a second. She was sorry there was a little trouble in paradise, but she had bigger issues, larger problems.

"Celeste, you are going to take your wonderful husband out to dinner. You hear me?"

"Yeah." Celeste chuckled. "You're right."

"Seriously, take him out for dinner and then enjoy your man."

"That's a thought. There hasn't been any romance stuff kicking off. I need to get on that, anyway."

"I am so sorry, Celeste." Simone glanced at her clock again. She wanted to hear Darius's voice. She needed to know if he thought of her in the hour she had left. Did she cross his mind at all? "I have a meeting in fifteen minutes. I've got to roll, girlie."

"No problem. I will keep you posted on how tonight goes."

Simone gently hung up the phone and stared at it. How desperate would that make her, to call him an hour and a half after spending an entire weekend with him? Besides, she needed to maintain space to be clear that this was not a formal relationship. His girlfriend had come by so she had to make sure she remembered he was not even hers. A text message. She could just send him a text. What if possessive girlfriend got her hands on it? No, calling would be better.

CHAPTER 34

Darius did not answer the phone. *Where could he be this early in the morning?* Simone thought, wondering whether he realized she had left and gone after his other woman. Maybe he wondered how long she would stay, when she would get the hint that she had overstayed her welcome. A wave of embarrassment washed over her. Had she embarrassed and played herself, taking his words literally and not understanding the difference between romantic lingo and love? The truth was that she was never really in the game. She always had a boyfriend; she had never had one-night stands and brief hookups. She never learned the rules of the casual dating game, not really. She thought she could figure it out, but Darius's words felt so real and true. Maybe she could not tell the difference between the lingoes of lust and allowed herself to buy into a romantic myth.

She fingered the cord of her office phone. She should not use this phone to call him. She did not need a record of her affair since the office taped all the phone calls. Still, she had to know whether she was just being an idiot. Whether the entire weekend had been a simple sexual release for him and she had lost her ability to separate. Maybe she would call just one more time. That would not seem desperate or stalkerish. She longed to hear the sound of his voice. It brought it all back. Even his scent. If he would just answer, say a word or two, she could linger on it for days.

She slowly dialed the house phone. She held her breath. She would only allow herself one call. Under no circumstances would she call any phone more than once within four hours. She thought that was reasonable. She already tried the cell. This call to the house phone was her last opportunity. She knew before dialing the number that if he did not answer, or if the conversation did not go well, she would feel down the entire day. That was how deep under her skin Darius had crawled. He felt like the fix she needed to get through the day on a pleasant vibe.

She remembered when he was a young boy with a crush. Big eyes that watched every move she made. He never looked away when she finally challenged him, meeting his eyes with a questioning smile. She remembered being surprised that his steady glance contained so much power. However, she considered him a young'un, like her little brother, Terence, although Darius was two years older than Terence. She just could not see him any different then.

Now they were grown. Darius was grown, and some kind of man he had grown into. Private. Powerful. Exuding physical prowess. Most amazing, still claiming that same crush he had years ago. It could all be a joke, though. He could be on the phone right now with his homeboys, laughing at the older woman who he turned out. He could be bragging about how he had her from behind, on her knees, or riding him as he sat on the floor, his back against the love seat. He was probably smirking at her that she had dissed him before and wanted for him now. Laughing that he would ever think a woman with stretch marks could be his caliber, especially with Miss Picture scaling the walls and breaking into his house to get to him.

Stop it, Simone. She had to silence the doubt. *Please answer the phone. Please. Please.* If he did not, then she was the joke.

The older woman he had to conquer to be rid of a childish crush. Simone held her breath as the phone rang and rang.

Simone slammed down the phone and leaned back into her chair. She wore the same outfit she had left work in on Friday. She hoped nobody noticed, but she actually could've given a damn. All she could think about was that this past weekend had been a huge mistake.

The phone rang, startling her. She answered it without checking, desperate to hear Darius's voice.

"Hello?"

"Simone?" The deep pitch of his voice confused her. She could not figure out why he sounded so muffled and strange.

"Yeah, you saw I called?"

"No," the voice hesitated, sounding clearer. "Actually, I am glad to hear that you did. I thought something was wrong when I couldn't get you this weekend."

The slight difference in tone finally clicked. Mr. Phone Lover. Smiling, she cupped the phone between her shoulder and ear. "Tim!"

"Oh, so now you remember me. I guess I wasn't the recipient of your earlier call, huh?"

Simone chose to ignore that question. "How are you?"

"I'm good. I am standing down in the lobby, heading to get some caffeine in me before this day gets rolling. I'm going in at ten. You wanna join?"

Simone hesitated, glancing down at her navy-blue suit jacket and skirt. She thought about Darius and Miss Picture, reuniting and enjoying Monday morning sex. "I am on my way down."

"Cool!"

CHAPTER 35

The house was dark. Empty and cold, there was no sign anyone had been there in days. The massive spider that weaved an incredible web every night and then removed it before dawn was working its way up and down its creation. Jackson shook his head. Simone tried to kill that spider so many times it was almost pathetic. Not only was she never able to accomplish it, but the spider also continued its ritual every time despite Simone. Had Simone been home the porch light would have been on, limiting the spider's efforts. It was clear it was in no fear of being caught. That was how Jackson knew the house was empty as soon as India dropped him off.

He hoped nothing bad had happened, but deep down, he was sure it had not. He always kept in close contact with his mother-in-law, especially when he was on travel and she had Jasmine. She and Jasmine were fine. *Where is my wife?*

When he stepped into the cool house, its stark emptiness struck him. It did not feel like their home, rather a shell of his life. There was no possible way Simone just did not come home unless something was wrong. He considered calling the police, but his instinct told him to wait.

No, this was different. If something were wrong, he would know. Simone's mother would have undoubtedly known. If he called once a day to speak with Jasmine, he could only imagine how many times a day Simone was in contact. No, she was trying to get his attention. She was upset about nothing lately. So, this was just her latest way to express herself. He would wait until she finally came home, express some love, make love to her, and everything would be all right.

That nagging suspicion she was cheating played around the corners of his mind. He stared at himself in the mirror, studying his eyes. When had he developed those slight bags and dark circles? Worrying about that mediation and sexual harassment case had taken its toll. Worrying about Simone and her never-ending unhappiness was wearing thin as well. However, he loved her, so he would tolerate it. She would snap out of it. He would fuck up, as usual. She would silently suck it up and self-destroy. Then she would come around. She always did.

He stripped out of his clothes, watching the Sean Jean slacks fall to the floor, with white stains around the opening. Jackson tossed his jacket on the bed and unbuttoned his shirt, tossing it to the floor next to his pants. He padded to the shower and turned the nozzle to hot. It took forever for the water to warm. *Damn, she hasn't even used the water here.* Jackson soaped himself down, scrubbing every inch and crevice. He could not find his shampoo, so he used the soap in his hair as well. The house felt so silent. He was not used to it. There was always music playing, a television blasting, Simone singing, Jasmine cooing. Sometimes, he tried to escape them and their daily noises by going to his office. Yet, today he longed for it, desperately wanted it. He needed his family.

He stayed in the shower long after he was clean, losing himself under the waterfall. Maybe it could rinse away his sins, his open weakness that made him unable to say no to any woman's offer. With closed eyes and leaning against the shower wall, thoughts consumed him. *Why did I have sex with Lynn? I have to admit, I was mesmerized. What in the hell was I thinking? What was I thinking with Nina? With any of them? What is wrong with me?*

Jackson stepped out of the shower and onto the thick, high pile rug in the middle of the bathroom. He wrapped Simone's thick, pink terrycloth towel around him. He had not expected it to smell like her, but it did. Not her exotic perfume smell, but her natural woman effervescence. Deeply he inhaled her smell. He wanted her there. He needed to lean his head against her chest and come clean about it all. She would forgive him, even if it took a while. She always did. It would be the first step to the new him. Admission. Laying across his bed, Jackson fell asleep.

A few hours later, sunlight trickled into the bedroom, sprinkling Jackson's face with warmth. He walked slowly to the kitchen. As Jackson walked past the telephone stand, his eyes landed on the ancient answering machine. He forgot about the house machine since Simone always checked it. He was certain she had left a message. He fumbled with it a while, wondering why she did not use voicemail. The play button did not seem to work until he realized he had to hold it down for several seconds. Jackson repeatedly listened to the messages from Celeste, Simone's mother, her brother, Terence, a few other friends and family, all wondering where Simone was and why she had not called them back. All wondering why she had disappeared, what had happened to their plans, if she was going to call them back, et cetera.

Jackson peeled out of the robe. He knew where she was. He would bet money her ass was at work. She never missed work, only for Jasmine would she even consider it. He was going down to her job to find out what in the hell was going on. What had she been doing for the past three days that caused her to drop off the face of the Earth?

Jackson threw on a button-down shirt and dress pants. At some point, he would have to go to the office today. The clothes he had stripped off earlier sat in a stinking pile in the middle of the floor, reeking of fishy snatch and weed. He threw the four-hundred-dollar suit in a plastic bag and tossed it into the trash. He kept the tie as a reminder of the hearing, Nina, Lynn, India, and the day his life felt like it was at its lowest point. He stepped into the garage, prepared to hop into his ride, and press his way into DC. He would confront Simone right in her office. He did not give a damn anymore. Where had she been when he was at his weakest? When he needed her the most? Where had she slept last night? *This shit is going to end today. I have no problem putting her ass out.* It was only when he stood in the middle of the empty garage that he remembered he did not have his car.

CHAPTER 36

He felt as if he was at the end of his rope. He did not even have a car and here he thought he was going to raise hell. No wonder Simone was cheating. How much more of an idiot could he be? Instead of worrying about getting to Simone, he still had to figure out a way to get to his car.

Jackson chuckled like a lunatic. "This is pathetic. I am pathetic. No, fuck that, I am still the man. I don't give a damn. I'm still going to find out what's going on." He whipped out his cell phone, pressed speed dial, and walked back into the house toward the kitchen.

"Yeah."

"Martia?"

"Yeah," she whispered.

"What are you doing?"

She hesitated. "I normally wouldn't answer this, but you are my boy. I am filming another client's husband getting his groove on."

"With?"

"Wife's sister. Always some sick shit. Anyway, what's up?"

"Some more sick shit." In the family room, he sat in Simone's favorite chair and inhaled her scent. The smell of her infuriated him more.

"Oh really?" He could hear the interest in her voice. "Who?"

"My wife." This time it slid off his tongue easily. His embarrassment was over. He needed to know what she was doing and how long she had been doing it. His indiscretions did not matter. He was a man. He was expected to creep, mess up, fix it, and try again. She was the mother of his child. Her ass had better not be cheating. The anger of the thought alone made his hand tremble.

"Oh. Are you sure?"

"Yep."

"Jackson, listen. Once you go down this road, there is no turning back. Do you understand that? Whatever I find could look worse than it is. Maybe you should—"

"Martia, thanks, babe, for always having my back. That's why I trust you with this. I know what I know and I need to know what I don't know."

Jackson stood up and paced the room. He did not want to push it. Martia could tell him no, but then what would he do?

"All right. Where can I find her?"

"Pennsylvania Avenue. Her offices are on Pennsylvania Avenue officially, but actually, it's on Thirteenth. The Bottsward Building. Seventh floor."

"Got it. I will give you a call in a couple of days."

"No, Martia, I need to know what you can find out now."

"All right, Jackson. Damn. All right. I will call you tonight."

Jackson closed the phone and slid it into his pocket. He needed to get to DC, find the tow company's location, and get back his ride. Then to the office to handle India and figure out how she was going to play it.

As Jackson dialed 411, the phone beeped. The firm's number popped up on the caller ID. The last person he wanted to speak to right now was India.

He flipped the phone open. "Jackson Woodson."

"Jackson, I have Mark Royster on the line." India's professional voice was clipped and cool. There was nothing to hint she had been out all night, cheating on her lover, caught her woman with her boss, cussed out her boss, or drove him around all night. "Are you available to take the call?"

Fuck her. I can be just as professional as she is. I can be just as cold as her "I just love one woman" bisexual ass.

"Jackson?"

"Concerning?"

"Clearance of a financial advance for a client."

Just what he needed. To deal with some bullshit from the sports law group. A call from Mark could only mean one thing: some athlete needed some emergency funds and he would have to put his name on the line until Mr. Millions covered his damn debts.

"Put him through."

"Hold, please."

Jackson sighed, wondering how long he and India were going to do this. He could not work with her as his enemy. He could not fire her, that much was for sure. Besides, he did not want her to be his enemy. Although he hated to admit it, he liked her. He would have to make this right.

"Mr. Royster, I have Mr. Woodson on the line."

They both waited for the click to signify India had hung up. Mark was one of the few lawyers at the firm he hung with outside of work.

"What's up, man?"

"Nothing at all. What about you?"

"Ah, the normal drama. I need your clearance to advance money on a client's account. Nick is out of town and you are the next in line for approval."

"Damn it, it's always something with your folks."

"I know." Mark chuckled. "That's why this is the best law to practice, baby. Pure contract law and babysitting. For millions. What's better than that?"

Now in the living room, Jackson leaned against the picture window. "Yeah, whatever man. Listen," He looked out over the front lawn. It was a beautiful neighborhood. Funny how the world could be crashing around him but everything on the surface remained the same. "I've gotten myself in a bit of a jam. My car was towed in DC. I wasn't even supposed to be in DC. Feel me?"

"Man, that's why I don't understand why y'all get married. It's not worth having to report to someone on my life."

"Yeah, yeah, yeah. Check it, I can't get down there to approve shit, is what I am trying to tell you. Not for another couple of hours."

"Naw, I got to come your way to meet with this client, anyway. The expenditure is for him, so I will scoop you up. You can come with me. We can get that part of it handled. Then I will bring you back to work with me."

He finally caught a break. "Cool. How boss do I have to get? A full meet the man suit or just my standard freshness?"

"Oh, you are hilarious. I think this brother wouldn't be impressed with too much flash. That's why he went with a law firm instead of a sports agency. Real down to earth."

"All right, I'll get ready. Remember to bring the paperwork."

"Yeah, I'll be there in half an hour."

"By the way, who is the client?"

"New cat. Just switched to us from ITG International. Darius. Darius Winfield."

CHAPTER 37

Mark had the sweetest Mercedes-Maybach S 560 Jackson had ever seen. *I need to upgrade, there is no doubt about that*, he thought as he slid into the soft, cream leather seat and faced Mark.

"Damn, you took long enough."

"What? Please, I know you ain't talking after losing your ride under circumstances you fail to disclose."

They laughed.

"This is cool. My boy doesn't live too far from here. Just down in Woodmore Estates."

"Cool."

Jackson tapped his hands on the wooden dash until he noticed his smudged fingerprints.

"Sorry, man."

"No worry. I'ma need your prints to ID you if you can't get this damn car situation of yours straight after Simone gets done with your ass."

"Tell me about it."

Within minutes, they pulled up to the iron gates, and the guard stepped out of the small wooden house. An older Black man, definitely retired from his day job, appraised the car, and his demeanor instantly relaxed.

"Gentlemen?"

"Yes, sir. Meeting my client, Darius Winfield."

"One second please, sir."

They watched the older man walk slowly back to the guardhouse, press a button, and talk for a few seconds. Then the gate slid open.

"I have always wanted to live in here," Mark said, watching the gate in awe.

Jackson chuckled. "Close your mouth, boy. You will have it soon. You need a wifey first, though."

"To hell I do."

The world behind them seemed to disappear as they rode down quiet streets overlooking man-made lakes, large estates, and golf courses.

"Damn, look at that house!" Jackson found it impossible to remain nonchalant. He had no idea the mansions in Woodmore Estates were so different from what he considered mansions in the normal neighborhoods. Lynn's house looked like an apartment compared to some of these gargantuan homes, with six- and seven-car garages, pools, and whole walls of windows. "Shit, I take it back. Your ass might not get in here any time soon."

They pulled into the back section of the neighborhood, down what initially appeared to be a driveway. As they moved forward, the driveway lengthened until the large house came into view. The house was not what Jackson was expecting. It looked like the houses they had already passed, nothing more exclusive.

"This brother paid a lot of money for this extra land for nothing, man. I would want people to see my joint."

Mark smirked. "That's the difference between this brother and us. Trust me. The last thing he wants is exposure or notoriety. He works hard to stay under the radar."

As they rolled up, they saw a man standing in one of the garages. He stepped out and pressed the remote control in his hand as he watched them park along the drive.

"D. Winfield. My man." Mark climbed out of his car and eased over to the man, giving him a pound before switching back into professional mode. "Darius, allow me to introduce you to Jackson Woodson, Senior Account Executive."

"Mr. Woodson, nice to meet you." Darius easily appraised him. "A money man, huh?"

"That would be me. Hope you don't mind my tagging along."

"Not at all. Come on in."

They walked next to Darius, who seemed a man of few words. As they entered the house, Jackson spoke. "Darius, I have actually met you before."

"Really?"

They walked together, side by side, with Mark walking behind, taking note of the house.

"Have you had this house appraised recently?"

"Of course, Mark. Damn." Darius laughed. "Your mind is a continuous calculator, huh?"

"Can't help it."

"So, where did we meet before?" Darius turned his attention back to Jackson as he motioned for them to sit on the large U-shaped sectional.

"When you were younger, in high school, you were good friends with my wife's brother. Well, she was my girlfriend then."

"Jackson Woodson. Of course." Darius stood there for a second, staring at him. For a brief second Jackson thought he spotted a slight smirk, but he must have been mistaken because, in the next second, Darius was shaking his head with his hands covering his face. "Oh, man. Damn."

Jackson watched as Darius's cool façade seemed to fade, he seemed sincerely shaken, and then he tried to pull himself back together.

"What was I thinking? Of course. Terence and I are still close, man, just don't get a chance to talk too often. How are you?" Darius reached over and hugged him. "So, so you married Simone."

At the mentioning of her name, a thick tension immediately fell over the room. Jackson could tell Darius was trying to sound light, but he could not help it. Jackson could not figure out what was going on. Then he remembered the puppy dog eyes Darius used to give Simone whenever he was around. *That's right. This boy had a lil' crush on her.*

"Yep, I married Simone. I believe it was the same weekend—"

"As my draft party. Yeah. I wanted her to come." Darius stared directly at him without blinking. Jackson winced a little, noticing he said *her* not them both. "And I hated that I missed the wedding."

"Yeah."

Mark plopped down on the other end of the sectional. Darius kept gazing at Jackson without blinking. Jackson had the feeling Darius wanted to say something but was weighing whether he should. Mark glanced between the two.

"See, Darius, had we known you had a connection with the firm, we could have had you a year ago, before ITG screwed up."

"Naw. I had to go down that path to see it wasn't for me, you know?" Darius finally turned away from Jackson and focused on Mark. "Can't tell a young'un that the agents are scavengers. We all believe they are the only way to the path of gold."

"Yeah."

"But I am a lot less trusting now, because of them. Lawyers or not, I know better than to blindly trust."

"Yeah." Mark coughed uncomfortably at that little nugget of truth and began digging through his bag. "Well, it's all good here."

"I hope so." Darius turned back to Jackson for a second and then looked at Mark. "So, how much involvement do you, or your department, have with my accounts."

Jackson thought he understood. Maybe Darius doesn't want a family friend with access to the numbers. That was why he was acting odd. It made sense to Jackson, got to keep personal from professional.

"Limited," Mark answered. "We are a firm, so money has to be properly accounted for. I can't just reach into your retainer for advancements without approval. Attorneys have a stricter code of ethics, and if we mess up, they yank our licenses. Without question. So, Jackson's department gets involved to approve advances, to make sure I am not dipping my hands in your money."

Darius nodded.

"So, here is the paperwork to affirm that you authorize this transaction. Sign here and here."

Darius picked up a heavy, gold-encased pen and signed.

"All right, so how do you want to handle this?"

"With as little fanfare as possible."

"Handle what?" Jackson asked.

Darius leaned back into the fluffy pillows and studied Jackson for a second. Jackson pulled at his tie, thinking, *This cat is definitely a different type of dude.*

"My girl caught me this weekend with my other."

"Aww, damn. So, I am not the only one with a weekend from hell."

"I don't know. I watched my girl climb onto my deck, unzip my patio cushion, and take out her own key to my home, man."

"Damn. I thought my woman drama was crazy."

"You got drama? A married man?" Darius leaned forward, a slight smile on his face as Mark laughed.

"This dude always got some woman drama. They can't leave his philandering ass alone." Mark laughed.

"Well, since we're sharing." Something in Jackson's gut stirred, a warning rang in his soul. He needed to keep his mouth shut. He had denounced cheating. It was a thing of his past. He had wanted to purge himself of that. He also wanted to prove himself. He did not need a National Football League contract and millions of dollars to pull women and have them following him. They wanted him anyway. He was player pimp enough, and he wanted Darius to know it. "I fired my jump off, and she tried to bring some action against me. Well, the lawyer representing me was a drop of pussy heaven. After the court stuff was handled yesterday, she took me back to her place and worked me out something unbelievable."

"Stop playing." Mark laughed louder. "No wonder your ass seemed so discombobulated this morning."

"Did you really just use the word discombobulated?" Jackson and Mark laughed.

Darius said nothing, just sat with that strange grin on his face.

"So, the lawyer was a freak, huh?" Darius asked.

"Yeah. This chick rode me every way possible. She did some shit I ain't never had done before. The kicker is, her lover walked in on us. My damn secretary."

"Oh shit!" Mark sat forward. "I've been trying to holler at India for weeks."

"Well, she claims she ain't gay or bi, but their asses are in love."

"What!"

Darius laughed aloud. "Damn, player, you had a crazier weekend than me."

"Yeah, but I'ma change my ways."

"Oh yeah? When you have that revelation?" Mark snorted.

"Last night." All three of them laughed, and Darius kept his eyes on Jackson.

"So, I need to bail shorty out?" Mark continued.

"Yeah. So, my girl, definitely an ex-girl, got drunk and acted a damn fool. Now she locked up and calling me for bail, but I am done with her."

"Hell yeah. She making keys and shit."

"More than that. I love my other girl."

"Aw, say it ain't so, playa." Mark bent over as if he had been shot.

"Yeah. I love her, man." Darius laughed easily and shrugged. "She's one of a kind. There's a situation, but I think I can help her out of that."

"Y'all are too much drama for me. That's why I stick and move." Mark stood up and did his best running back shake. "Stick and move."

"How're you gonna help her out of her situation? You ain't thinking about nothing crazy, are you?" Jackson decided that Darius might be a touch crazy. "You can have any woman you want and you're messing with one with a situation? Better leave that alone."

"Naw. He gave himself away on a platter. Nothing much for me to do."

They sat in silence. Jackson felt a little uncomfortable, but could not put his finger on why.

Mark chimed in. "She must be something to make her worth the hassle. I've tasted that before but I lost her. I ain't mad at ya, D."

Darius reached over and gave him a pound while Jackson stared at Mark in wonder.

"You want some lunch? My woman made some chicken curry with rice. Everything she makes is like butter, baby. You want?"

Mark shook his head. Jackson did not answer at all. Maybe he should have kept his little story to himself, now that they were talking about women worth hanging onto. He couldn't talk about this past weekend and now talk about how wonderful his wife was. It would seem disingenuous or expose him for the asshole he really was. He remained silent.

"So, what is our mission then?" Mark continued, but Darius ignored him, continuing to stare at Jackson.

"You know, you got lucky, man. Simone, she is a keeper, too."

"No doubt." Jackson dropped the light facial expression and stared coldly back at Darius. He did not want another man talking about his wife.

"We're both just trying to get what you got," Darius continued. "You can understand that, right, playa?"

"Well, your ass is," Mark interrupted. "Shit, I am out of the game. I lost mine, won't find another."

Darius did not look at Mark, his eyes still locked onto Jackson.

Jackson did not care for him. He did not like the fact that he had not spoken about his wife and Darius had mentioned her, making him seem like a chump. He did not like the quiet inside joke that Darius seemed to be having at his expense. He did not like how he felt so uncomfortable and could not explain why. He did not like that Darius knew his wife at all, that a weird, thick tension invaded the room every time Darius mentioned her. He was ready to go.

Jackson stood up. "Well, it's been real. We better head back."

"Yeah. Where do you want me to take her?" Mark asked again.

"Back to her place. Don't bring her here. Make sure she doesn't put on a show or talk to the media or anything. Knowing her, the news crews will be waiting at the damn jail to record her jailbreak."

Mark laughed, but Jackson started walking to the door.

"Jackson, it was good seeing you again." Darius followed him.

"Yeah, you, too." Jackson quickly made his way out of the house, deciding to wait for Mark in the car.

"Shit," Mark said, climbing behind the wheel of his Benz, ten minutes later. "What was that about?"

"I should have kept my little stories to myself. I don't need any more of my dirt getting to my in-laws."

"Naw, Darius ain't that type. Trust me."

Jackson did not answer as he stared at Darius standing on the front steps of the house, watching them pull out. Darius watched him closely until they were out of the large yard. Jackson instinctively knew he would not be welcomed back.

CHAPTER 38

The pounding in her head grew louder and louder, and the stench all around her was overwhelming. Under no circumstances should she have been in these conditions. This was Darius's fault.

The other girl in the cell sat against the opposite wall, her eyelids drooping. The girl had not spoken all night and had not moved off that bench for hours, and neither had Tiffany. She sat for hours, wondering whom to call. She could not call her mother for some ignorant mess like this, and she knew Lindsey did not have enough money to bail her out. So, after hours of her pride wasting away, she broke down and called Darius.

He did not answer the first few times. She rolled her eyes and breathed hard, trying to figure out how she could get in touch with him. The payphone number was a strange one, there was no way he would answer it. The guard leading her back to the cell wanted her. It was easy to tell. If he had anything going for him, other than a pathetic nine-to-five for no more than fifty grand, she would have no problem hitting him off. He was fine as hell, that much she had to admit.

He turned out to be so much easier than she thought.

"What's up?"

She glanced up, pretending to be surprised he had spoken to her.

"I don't belong here."

"No one does, right?"

"No, I am Darius Winfield's fiancée. If the media finds out I am here, they could ruin my life."

He leaned forward, barely seated on the edge of the metal chair.

"It's just a holding cell. It's not like you're in jail."

Tiffany lowered her chin, pursed her lips, raised her brows, and looked him. Tiffany shook her head. "You don't understand. He is going to go crazy when he finds out I am in here and couldn't reach him."

"What, you couldn't get through?"

She shook her head. "He doesn't recognize the number."

"Well, he ain't gonna recognize no number up in here." He leaned back in the chair with both legs stretched out in front of him, observing her. "You're fine as hell."

"Thank you."

"So that's you, huh?"

"Yeah."

"He got it sewed up?"

Tiffany batted her eyelashes, wanting to laugh. Like a simple jail guard could compare to Darius. "Yeah, he lays it down."

They sat in silence for a minute. She looked over at the girl whose eyes were drooping.

"That's that heroin." The guard answered Tiffany's unspoken question. "That's why she's tripping like that."

"I need to get out of here." Tiffany stared at the floor. Fear crept into her for the first time. She did not realize she was locked in a cell with someone tripping off drugs. "Can you send Darius a text, please? Tell him I am here."

"Uh-uh. Now you're tripping. The last thing I need is for him to report me or something. That's my job."

"But—"

"Uh-uh."

It had taken her a couple of hours, but he finally did it. Darius responded to the text immediately. So now, she sat waiting, wondering how to explain the mess she had gotten into. How to spin it so he would see it was his fault for all the pain he caused her.

Her new boyfriend moved her to the bench next to his desk when she kept watching the heroin junkie. Tiffany sat there, trying to smooth her hair down and adjust her clothes. She was still sporting the sweats from two days before when she had channeled a Spiderman vibe, trying to scale the walls into Darius's house.

She and Lindsey had gone for drinks at Crossroads, a Caribbean nightspot. Since she was dressed so casually, she tried to keep a low profile in the corner. The rage in Darius's eyes, as he protected whomever he was screwing, felt like a dagger in her heart. She could not get over it, him holding a death grip on her arms, as if he could and would willingly break them. Somebody had slid into her spot and she was hotter than fish grease. So, they drank and drank.

Men sent drinks to her and Lindsay and they swallowed those down like fruit juice. Then they decided to switch nightspots and head into DC. They tried to stroll into Lounge 201 but were instantly stopped when Tiffany's sneakers and sweats caught the attention of the bouncer. As she argued with him, she spotted a Ford Explorer, the same one she saw in Darius's three-car garage. When the truck stopped, two Black women climbed out. Tiffany waited, calling Darius repeatedly on his cell, but he refused to answer. When the women disappeared into the club, she and Lindsey took bricks out of Lindsey's truck and smashed all the windows. The bricks had originally been planned for Darius's house, just in case. Had they not been so drunk, they would have noticed security. Lindsey got away, screaming and running into an alley, but Tiffany was having too much fun to stop. She was dragged downtown.

"Tiffany Lawson, your bond has been posted." Her new boyfriend smiled down at her, leaning in close. She smiled back. She would give him her number. He could be a jump-off or a late-night creep. Why should she deny herself so much male beauty when Darius had no loyalty to their relationship? She kissed him quickly on the cheek, smoothly so no one else saw, mumbling words about her calling him, and walked into the front reception area. Darius was nowhere in sight. Instead, she spotted two, uptight-looking men, probably attorneys. Both looked like hoes.

"Ms. Lawson, I'm Mark Royster, Mr. Winfield's attorney. I am here on his behalf."

Tiffany snorted and rolled her eyes. "So, he sends you two, huh? Darius didn't even come himself."

"No, he had an important meeting with a potential sponsor so he asked that I make sure you get home safely."

"Meaning he's trying to cover himself without me making a public scene. Did he mention what he did to me? Huh?"

There were other people in the room and both men recognized Tiffany would get louder the more witnesses she had. "Ms. Lawson, why don't we get you in the car?"

"No, look at this." She pointed to her arm and severe black and blue marks. "He did this. I threatened to find out who his little girlfriend was, and this is what he did to me. I could press charges."

"Ma'am—"

"I got her plate, too. Her little Ford Explorer being hidden in the back of the garage don't mean nothing."

"Listen. If you want a ride, you will lower your voice and act like you've got some common sense. I have no problem leaving your wild ass here." Mark's nice-guy demeanor changed quickly.

"Excuse me?"

"Jackson, we're out."

"Leave then."

Mark grinned at her, and then called her bluff by spinning on his heels while Jackson stared at her. She had not signed out yet. She could not leave without them. Jackson shrugged and turned to follow Mark.

"Wait! Wait, I didn't mean to vent. I just can't believe he's playing me like this."

"Ma'am, I don't know the arrangement between you and Mr. Winfield. I am just doing my job." Mark fussed back and forth with Tiffany for a few minutes, while she received her things and signed out.

Jackson sat in the back seat, and she noted he kept her in his line of sight while Mark drove. They rode in silence until they pulled up to her apartment building in Alexandria, Virginia. As she climbed out, she rolled her eyes at Mark.

"Take care," he said with a smile.

"Whatever," she snarled. Just as she started to slam the door closed, she heard Jackson speak up.

"One question for you. What color was the Ford Explorer you saw? The plate? Do you remember?"

CHAPTER 39

Before stepping off the elevator, Simone shifted her skirt. The tiger-eyed Tim stood across the lobby near the magazine stand. She strolled over to him, walking slowly and unfazed. Tim was such a pro that she always attempted to seem nonchalant in his presence. Her hips ached and she could not help but think about Darius. Smiling, she waved at Tim.

"Hey, sexy."

Simone laughed lightly. "Right back at you, sexy."

"Yeah, I needed five minutes in your presence today. I knew I made the right call."

"Where are we heading for coffee?"

"My place?"

"No, I don't think so."

"All right, I'll settle for Starbucks."

"Definitely."

"Where were you this weekend?"

"Just getting some R and R."

"R and R bullshit. You are glowing."

"Am I?"

"Yes, you are." He held the door for her as they stepped out into the sunshine. "What's got you glowing like a fly in shit, beautiful?"

She shrugged and smiled.

"Aw. So, someone got their swerve on this weekend."

"No, no—"

"Simone."

"Yes."

"Simone."

"Yes."

They fell out into laughter, she resting her hand on his forearm. She adored him and enjoyed his company. However, she had someone else on her mind, and not even Tiger Tim could dissuade her.

"You know, we could take off the rest of the day, have a romantic lunch."

"No. I can't, Tim, but I appreciate the asking."

"You've got me wanting to taste a little."

"Damn, you can talk dirty in the morning, too." Simone laughed, covering her mouth and wrinkling her nose.

"Trust me. You haven't even begun to scratch my surface."

"Uhm. Stop setting me up to answer you with things I am not about to say one block from my job in the morning."

"I am addicted to your voice."

"Really? I am addicted to your eyes."

"Really?" He seemed genuinely surprised. "What's keeping you from me, Simone?"

She smiled and shrugged.

He turned his back to her and ordered coffee. As they waited, his fingertips gently brushed her hips, just lightly enough not to be obvious.

"Stop—"

"What's keeping you from me, really?" They secured a booth. "You're husband?"

"No." She almost choked on the coffee in an attempt to keep from laughing. "Definitely not."

"Then what?"

She sighed. It was time to get serious. "We have to cool it down for a minute. I am kind of in a thing and I can't do this, too."

"'Kind of in a thing'? Someone scooped in and took my spot?"

"No, someone from my past returned. You can understand that."

"Yeah, I can." He shook his head. "It doesn't stop me from doing this." He reached under the table and caressed her knee.

Simone smiled seductively at him. She could play and flirt with Tim and his tiger-eyes all day. Being around him made her feel more feminine and alluring. Still, she wasn't going to go any further with him. It was bad enough she was so different, had changed so much. She didn't know what she thought about herself and the new men in her life. What type of woman did that make her? What type of mother? Darius had captivated her heart and her mind. The only part of her that was not his was the part wrestling over how to deal with Jackson. How could she leave him without hurting Jasmine? The baby loved her father, how could she cause her pain? The thought had consumed her mind lately. If she could wrap herself into Darius for eternity, she would. His love felt so safe and steady. She wanted to give herself completely over to it.

In the spirit of flirting, Simone leaned closer to Tim. "All right. It doesn't stop me from doing this." Simone lightly ran her hands across his lap.

"Whew!" Tim shot back in his seat, an incredulous expression on his face that made Simone laugh. "Girl, you'd better stop playing up in here."

"I'm sorry, I couldn't help myself."

"Uh-huh. See, all those phone rendezvous have got you curious." He tapped the table, staring at her.

"No. You always had me curious. Maybe one day."

"Maybe. In the meantime, I'm still calling you. I enjoy the sound of your voice."

"Me, too, Tim. Me, too."

Simone and Tim teased and flirted until he walked her back to the elevator banks. Tim insisted on waiting for the elevator to come.

"So, can I get a kiss goodbye?"

"Uhm. Maybe if we weren't in my office building."

"Okay. See, you've got me begging." Tim glanced around the empty lobby. "There's no one here."

"There's always someone here. Even when you can't see them."

He stood close behind her, so the small hairs on her neck stood up. "I'm glad you came down. I needed to see you."

"Always. Whenever you call, I will be here."

"For real?"

"For real."

The bell on the elevator rang. "I'll call you soon." Before Simone could turn to respond, he wrapped his arm around her waist and kissed the back of her neck.

Chuckling, she shook her head and stepped on the empty elevator. Turning around, she smiled at him as he backed away. Of course, she had told him about her spot. "You are too much."

"You know it."

CHAPTER 40

B uried under work for the past few hours, Simone
worked through lunch to make up for her morning
coffee with Tim. Besides, she needed to focus on
something other than the hurricane of confusion her life
had become. The guilt threatened to overwhelm her at any
moment, followed by acute embarrassment. She did not want
to be out there again, dating and wondering what if and why
not.

She stared at the schematics in front of her. The building
designs were turning into a blur before her eyes. She was
responsible for supervising all aspects of the building and
offered building support and resources to the firms contained
within. With the advanced surveillance equipment, she could
see any room in the building at any time, which was why she
told Tim someone was always watching. That someone was
under her control and the last thing she needed was her staff
watching her getting felt up.

Unlike the men who dominated her field, Simone
maintained her sexuality and femininity, performing her job
in a classy manner. She gained the respect of all the women
in the building, wearing her stylish suits as she trained new
employees on building security and etiquette or approved
layout for new office space and building code issues. That was
one aspect of her life where her dad had played an important
part.

Simone was MacArthur "Mac" Sheridan's firstborn. Overlooking she was a girl, he designed toy buildings, racing toy cars, and enjoyed all of his hobbies with her. She participated in athletics, was the star sprinter, and a good basketball player. Mac had always been there, coaching, encouraging, leading, and supporting her. Until her body began to change. One day, she returned from the hairdresser blowing on her freshly, manicured nails. Mac looked at her and it seemed like he had spotted a stranger. Afterward, he kept his distance. Her mother always waved him off, said he could not handle that she had changed. However, Simone felt abandoned.

That empty feeling reminded her of Jackson. It was how she felt all the time lately. She had not thought about her father in so long, had not thought about how painful each day had been until she had been able to escape and go to college. She hated growing into a woman at first. She thought her breasts were something hideous, her widening hips were evidence of her body betraying her. The changes had cost her a best friend. Her father. He deferred to her mother on everything after that, not wanting to engage at all.

I married a man just like my father, she thought, wondering, had she been so blind? It was so obvious. They were so similar; needing her as she engaged in their worlds, and participated in what they wanted, but ignoring her completely regarding her needs. Clueless yet selfish. Calculating and lazy. Her father and Jackson.

The emptiness that rocked her pit made her drop her pencil. She needed some comfort, someone to tell her she was pretty and lovely. Someone who wanted to be in her company. She needed someone who wanted to sit and watch her cook, enjoy her feminine wild, instead of trying to deny it, shape it, or ball it up into a neat, compact circle. She needed Darius.

Simone glanced at the clock. It was 4:12 p.m. She dialed his number. He had not returned her earlier call, but she did not want to think about it. If he did not answer, she would not play herself and call him back again. She would call Tim. Any man who could breathe desire into her was eligible.

"You called." He answered on the first ring.

Simone laughed. "I called."

"What are you doing?"

"Thinking about you." There was no need to be coy or shy. The need within her burned so acutely and the passion she had shared with Darius had been so intimate, she dropped the façade and got straight to the point.

"I'm glad to hear it. I just got in from working out."

"Are you tired out?"

"No. Not for you. What do you have in mind?"

"I need one mo' 'gain."

"Word?" Darius chuckled in her ear. If one thing she learned from Tim, men did not mind her directness on the phone. "You're welcome to whatever you need. You coming over?"

"Is it all right?"

"Simone," he hesitated. "Woman, you just don't know. Hell yeah, it's all right."

Simone forgot he was younger than her, forgot about the little boy that used to stare at her in admiration. Darius was a man, a full-grown, fully capable man, and he was the only man that filled all the gaps in her inner core.

"No, Darius. You don't know. You've got me confused. In love. In lust."

"I know one thing. You don't have to ask to come over. You don't have to ask me to be with me. Just stay with me."

Simone remained silent.

"Can you do that?"

"I want to."

"Come on over here. I'm waiting for you."

Simone put the phone down. She did not know how much time she could buy. Her mother was keeping Jasmine another day so she could take her to church that night. She wanted a chance to show off her grandbaby. Simone figured she had at least five or six hours. Jackson always came in late at night from travel.

She tucked her papers away and organized her desk. After leaving a message for her assistant, Simone stood up to leave before realizing she had on the same clothes Darius had seen her in. *Oh, it doesn't matter*, she thought initially but realized it did matter. *Got to keep the spark brand new.* Simone would stop by her house on the way to Darius's to freshen up, but she didn't want to. She didn't want to waste any extra time. She thought it best to call India to get Jackson's schedule. Simone was cutting it a little too close for comfort. She had to make sure she was home before he returned, but she was not going to deny herself. She was just going to risk it. *Fuck him. Didn't he say I wasn't woman enough for him or something like that?* That slowed down her panic. She was not going to have dinner cooked or a warm bed for him. She was so used to the routine that she needed to be there.

Running out of the office, Simone quickly spoke, "Call Jackson at office," into her iPhone.

"Hello, Mr. Woodson's office."

"Hi, India, it's Simone."

By the long deliberate pause, Simone assumed India had not heard her properly.

"India? Hello? You there? It's Simone Woodson."

CHAPTER 41

India stared at the digital display on her office phone. The firm had updated to this new technology, the fancy screen and screen saver with multiple options. The vivid caller ID, identifying the caller's name, time, and the last time they called within the past twenty-four hours. This was the first call from this number in over a month. Simone. Simone Woodson. She must be on her cell. It's a 202 area code.

India considered not answering it, but that was the other problem with this new technology. It made it easier for the bosses to track them. Missed calls could mean lost business, which was the equivalent of flushing money down the toilet. So missed calls were investigated. If she were not at her desk, the call would be forwarded. There were so many checks and protocols, so many routines and formulas for every minutia of her day.

"Mr. Woodson's office. India Walker speaking."

"Hi, India. This is Simone."

For a second, India shook her head. Was karma testing her? Checking on how vindictive or hateful she was, how much confusion could she put into the atmosphere? Had she not been teased and frazzled enough for today.

"India? Hello? You there? It's Simone Woodson."

"Of course. Hi, Simone. Please accept my apologies. It has been an incredibly difficult day."

"I'm sorry to hear that. I hope you are okay?"

She's sweet, India thought, shaking her head. What was wrong with this woman? She was so easy, caring, and concerned in every interaction. Didn't she have any barriers or hedge of protection around her emotions? *No wonder Jackson dogs her so easily. It's like a gazelle with a lion.*

"I'm fine, thanks for asking." India could hear her tone loosening, sounding friendlier. She liked Simone but found it hard to respect a woman who needed a man so much that she tolerated anything from him. Did Simone not have any self-respect, any dignity? Had she not been taught about self-empowerment, or was her entire definition the accomplishments of Jackson? Then again, who was she to judge?

"India, I know Jackson was supposed to return from travel tonight. Do you know what time?"

There it was. The question India was trying to avoid. The ultimate test. She could jackknife Jackson's whole world right here, right now. She could make him experience the pain she felt when she walked into her beautiful home to find him defiling her only true love. She could repay him a million times over with such an innocent statement, one for which she would never be blamed. Something like, "Oh, he actually returned from travel two days ago. You haven't talked to him?" Or, "Actually, he's already here. He just completed the mediation for the sexual harassment charge against him."

"India, you there?"

Then again, Jackson could jack her world, too. Lynn seemed different this morning, removed from her. Lynn had found something in Jackson she liked, although it also disgusted her. Lynn said she and Jackson were the same.

Selfish and manipulating. Whoever messed with them was bound to be hurt. Was that true? Was Simone no more than Lynn trying to love someone whose very definition of love was vague and uncertain? India suddenly felt sad, and she recognized one other thing. Jackson could kill her career. If she messed with his wife and family, he could tarnish her name throughout the legal community. He had the ties. He would use his connections to destroy her if she crossed the line. Not only that, he could out her. She would catch it from both straight and lesbian women. No one liked a line straddler. No one could respect that. Everyone expected her to fit into a neat box and Jackson could use her inability to do so to rock her world.

"Simone, sorry for the delay, I was just checking his schedule. I am not sure what time he is due back this evening. He sent a message earlier that he had an unexpected layover. I will send a message to his cell—"

"No, no. Don't worry about it. It's not like he will notice whether I am there or not anyway." Simone let out a little laugh, which scraped against India's feelings as if she had run her nails across a chalkboard. Her light statement held so much pain. "I am going to stay at my mother's tonight. If he contacts you before I speak to him, can you give him the message?"

"Definitely."

"Oh, and India…"

"Yes."

"I know your day will get better, although you seem a little down. You are a good person. Goodness will always come your way. Talk to you soon."

Simone disconnected the call, leaving India in deep thought.

CHAPTER 42

They rode in silence, Mark tapping the steering wheel as he drove. Jackson did not look at him, his eyes locked on the glass plate in front of him. The cinnamon-colored woman, whose name escaped his mind, had come close to shattering his entire world. She did not remember the plate, but she knew the color of the Ford Explorer. He had not even had to explain why he asked, Mark could probably put two and two together.

It could not have been Simone. It just could not have been. All this time he was handling his wife, leading her with her nose wide open, only to think she had a pro football player. A pro football player? How could he compete with that? With that monstrous house, enormous, exclusive land. The fame. The bling. The shine. If anything, it proved she was laughing at him. Holding contempt for him, using him, and laughing at him behind his back. They probably both were. *That was why that punk sat there all smug, running up in my wife and laughing at me.*

He wanted to slap the taste out of Simone's mouth, but he knew better. He had never laid a hand on a woman, and he would not start today. *I'm leaving. My baby girl is coming with me.* He knew that was not happening either. There was no way Simone would let Jasmine go anywhere she did not control or rule, other than her mother's house. He had been around lawyers enough to know that infidelity did not amount to an unfit parent for a mother. The fact that she was less than a tramp would be irrelevant when it came to issues of custody. Of course, she would throw his infidelity up in his face. Who would punish a woman scorned?

Jackson sighed heavily and nestled back in the seat. Mark pulled into the garage that held his towed car.

"Thanks, man."

"No problem." As Jackson climbed out of the car, Mark stopped tapping. "Listen, man…"

Jackson walked around to the driver's side of the car.

"Listen, I know what you're thinking. You're tripping man. No way. No way is that happening."

"Why not?" Jackson felt his anger rising. He was embarrassed now. Humiliated that someone knew his situation. "You don't think Simone would? Shit—"

"Listen, there is no way. He wouldn't sit there and toy with you like that? Simone wouldn't get with him, anyway. Stop tripping."

"I know one thing. I might need a lawyer real soon."

"Just like that?" Mark pounded his fist on the steering wheel. "Jackson, that's some bullshit. A man that knows your wife's family has a girlfriend with the same color truck and that's it, you're just leaving? After all your dirt?"

Jackson stared at Mark.

Now Mark's brow was furrowed as if he were equally upset. "You're pimping this one and that one, although you're married. Everyone knows, including your wife, and she stays faithful and loyal to your whoring ass. Then you hear some speculation and you're talking divorce." Mark shook his head. "You're married. That's why you married, committed ones blow my mind, man. You're talking about leaving and you've got a daughter. A daughter. Your daughter is going to be raised by another man. Because you thinking about doing something crazy that's going to make your wife leave you even if she ain't cheating. What if she did cheat? Like you don't deserve that. Like you ain't have it coming."

"Listen, keep your mouth out of grown folk's business, son."

"I've got your 'son.'" Mark's door flung open, causing Jackson to jump back. "I have watched you for years, running the streets, even trying to hang with me. I don't have a Simone at home. A child to protect. If I did, you think I would risk it over the bullshit you're playing with? About to mess up your livelihood, messing with Nina? Not even out of the mediation and banging the lawyer. Then you tripping like this? I got your son, da—"

Mark's phone rang while Jackson stared at him, amazed Mark was about to swing on him. Mark didn't have to, his words sunk into Jackson's skull, into his core.

He held both hands up. "Mark, calm down, man. I hear—"

"Naw, fuck that. I'm sick of your bullshit, man. Sick of the way you live your life. Do you know why I am not married? Because I respect marriage. I respect that it's a unity between a man, his wife, and God. God, son. Is there any God in you? I mean, any? You're like a heathen. How are you gonna play with God's institution and think good can come out of it? If Simone is banging that dude, that's on you, man. You led her there. I have loved, and I lost her. I lost her. You ain't never even asked, although I mention it all the time."

"I know, you said you lost her. I figured you got busted or had an argument—"

The power of Mark's hand slamming into his jaw caused him to stumble backward. With equal force, another jab in his gut bent him over. He was not going to hit Mark back, although it took all his restraint as he began to feel nauseous. He ducked a couple of more blows and took a few steps back.

"Yo, you are way out of line! Calm down."

"Fuck you!" Mark stumbled back against his car, his hands over his face. "She died. I wasn't a whore like you. We didn't argue. We didn't have reason to. Her name was Gabriella, not that you ever asked. She died carrying my baby. In the middle of the night, she just died. Lying next to me."

"I didn't—"

"Yeah, I know your selfish ass didn't know. Because you don't care about nothing but you and getting your next nut."

They stood there for a moment, Jackson bent over trying to catch his breath and Mark with his hand over his face.

"I'm out," Mark said suddenly. Just like that, the emotion disappeared, the stone face returned. The person Jackson had always taken for granted. He had never seen that many emotions in Mark, had never dug deeper. Mark started the car, rolled up his window, and glanced at his cell phone as he slowly pulled forward. Jackson watched, making sure Mark was not about to run him over. Instead, Mark slammed on the brakes with a screeching halt and rolled the window down.

"By the way," he said with a barking laugh. "Ya boy, Darius, just sent me a text message. He's dropping the firm. Let's see how you explain this one away. You just cost the firm millions, *son*. Guess that answers your questions about him and Simone, doesn't it?" With that said, he pulled away.

CHAPTER 43

S imone sat in her car while it idled, wondering whether she should go inside. She could not deny herself, as much as she tried. A grin spread across her face. At least one more night of bliss, of sexual heaven before she had to pull herself away and detox, refitting back into a decent mother and human being. Being a decent wife was very low on her list of priorities. After all, her husband had questioned her womanhood and treated her as if she were a doormat. Why should she keep sacrificing to be faithful to him?

The front door opened. She wondered how long he would let her sit out here in thought, especially with that state-of-the-art security system he had. He stepped out onto the wide brick platform.

"Hey, babe."

She loved the sound of his voice, like warm liquid pouring over her. She smiled.

"What are you sitting out there doing?"

"Thinking."

He nodded, and then took a few more steps near the car.

"You were thinking about me?"

"No doubt." Simone grinned harder, feeling the dimples in her cheek. He reached for the car and opened the door. Simone sighed. There was no turning back now.

Darius kissed her forehead and each of her eyelids. He lightly held her hands in his. "I missed your smell."

Simone stifled a groan. Just like that, he had her open. Just like that.

His strong arms wrapped around her as he hugged her tightly. "Hmmm. I'm glad you came back to me." He slowly moved her toward the house, keeping her closely pressed in an embrace with his warm arms. At the front door, Darius dropped down to his knees, easily sweeping her blouse out of the waistband of her skirt and kissing her hip.

Simone squealed. She never knew the side of her hip was so sensitive. Her nipples protruded through her blouse and her bra, her temple vibrated and throbbed.

"I love the feel of your lips."

"I know," Darius muttered, between kisses. "I will put them anywhere you want them."

"Really?"

"Tell me where."

"Right here." Simone pointed to her belly button and watched in delight as he obliged, stroking his tongue around the circle of her belly before planting kisses around her.

Simone slid her skirt up and pointed to her upper thigh. "Right here."

"I like that." Darius lightly bit the side of her upper thigh and sucked on it while she rubbed his head.

She tapped his shoulder. "What about right here?" Simone laughed lightly, pointing to the space between her breasts.

"Now you're talking. You know what I like." Darius pulled her closer, unbuttoning the blouse with his teeth and lightly licking the hollow between her breasts. He held a breast in each hand, kneading it, rubbing it, and lightly stroking her nipples in tune with the rhythm of his tongue.

"Damn, Darius." Simone placed her hands over his, following his motion.

"You know what?" He moved back a little.

"What?"

"I want to see you touch yourself."

"Right here, in the foyer?"

"Naw, come here."

Darius grabbed her hand and led her through the marble columns entering the kitchen, through the high arched doorway to the back staircase. Instead of going up, he led her downstairs to a section of the house she had not seen before.

"Where are you taking me?"

"Sauna."

"Why?"

"I want to see you sweat." His statement was so definite and without shame. She loved how comfortable he was in his skin. "I want to taste you, lick off every drop of water you produce."

"You make me sweat. Over and over again."

They walked down a long hallway, past the bar and barstools, the pool table, and the large, dark movie theater room.

"Wait, wait. I want to go in there." Simone pulled away from him, pushing open the double glass doors. Darius followed her, smiling and watching her take in the movie screen the length of the entire wall. "It's soundproof?"

Darius nodded.

Simone gasped at the heavy, gold, velvet curtains on either side of the projector, the shelves of DVDs and video games. The soft leather couches looked like buttercream and the heavy, gold frames contained movie posters. The wall unit contained a small stereo system. Simone walked over to it and stared. She did not dare touch a Black man's stereo. The music started, and she jumped a little at the sudden sound. Darius waved the remote control at her. She held her hands out. He shook his head and smiled, placing the remote in his pants.

She shook her head in time with the music. Darius made her forget all of her insecurities. Dancing, she swayed her hips to the slow, heavy beat. Darius stood against the far wall, watching her and smiling. She had stripped a million times to music in her bathroom, but never with an audience. Closing her eyes and humming to the music, she slowly stepped out of her skirt and slipped out of the blouse. Her sensitive nipples made her jump at her own touch. She was thankful she had on her lace bra and panties set. She hummed and closed her eyes again, allowing the music to cover her like thick honey, imagining the sweet rhythm pouring all over. With one hand, she stroked her breast while she slid the other down to her thigh.

Still moving slowly, she pressed her fingers against her swollen temple, the instant pressure causing her to gasp in delight. Simone ran her hands up and down her stomach, dragging her fingertips up to her neck and then back down to her nipples. Simone returned her right hand to her thigh as she parted her legs. She reached her hand further in, feeling her moistness on her fingertips.

Opening her eyes, Simone realized Darius was gone. She stopped and spun around in a circle. She barely saw the wide projector screen, the other wall full of panels, and the stereo system. Had he left to keep from laughing?

"Babe, I'm right here." He was sitting on the second level of raised, buttercream couches, his head against the headrest with his legs straight out in front of him. His hand was stroking his massive erection. For a second, she almost closed her eyes and looked away. Then she wanted to laugh. He was that turned on by her? Why had she never noticed he was that large before?

Simone stared at him and then smiled.

"Look how you got me." He looked down at himself and stood up, his power pointing straight at her.

Resuming her seductive dance, she smiled. "Come look at how you got me."

He walked to her, and she placed his hand underneath hers as she slowly widened her legs and slid his hand between the warmth of her thighs. They both sighed at the touch, and his warm mouth completely covered hers, his tongue licking every inch of her mouth. The kiss felt so deep and overwhelming that Simone almost lost her balance when Darius pulled away.

"Look." He motioned over her shoulder to the large projector where an enlarged image of her with Darius's hand stroking her, met her. Immediately embarrassed, she looked back at him.

"Take me off that thing."

"Can't you see how beautiful you are? Look at it. I was watching you, then watching the screen, then watching you. Look at you, babe." Placing his other hand under her chin, he lifted her head. "Look at us. Look at how we look together."

Simone glanced shyly at the screen, determined to keep her eyes focused on him and not herself. The hidden voyeur in her was excited, interested as she watched herself on the screen, reaching out and lightly running her fingers across his erection. The sight of him swaying, inhaling, and seeming weak on the large platform heightened her excitement.

"You're so wet."

"Only for you, babe."

Without warning, his hands were on her hips, lifting her onto the nearest loveseat against the wall. He placed her bottom on the headrest, her back against the cold wall. Kneeling in the seat, he held himself in one hand while using the other to widen her thighs. She reached a hand over her head to brace the wall for balance, but before she could catch her breath, his tongue was plunging in and out of her, licking up and down her inner sanctum, pulling on her outer lips, flicking against her engorged clitoris.

He looked up. "Open your eyes," Darius whispered throatily. "Watch me. Watch how much I love pleasing you."

Simone met Darius's eyes before his head disappeared again between her thighs. The jolt of pleasure caused her to throw her head back and groan, but she wanted to see. She slowly looked at the projector, saw her naked body on top of the huge leather loveseat, his hand resting on her thigh, his head bobbing between her thighs. She stared at his massive back, the perfect ass, the wide shoulders, and the back of his thick thighs. He was so beautiful. She was amazed by how beautiful it all seemed, with her coffee brown legs against the warm, buttercream brown contrasted with his wheat complexion.

Watching herself, she placed her hand on her breast and lightly squeezed her nipple. Too overcome to care about maintaining her grip on the wall, she rubbed her breasts as he squeezed her thighs, flexing the walls of her sex in perfect rhythm with his tongue. She never closed her eyes, amazed by the sexual creature in front of her that seemed so in power and at one with her. The explosions erupted deep within, and she closed her eyes, clinging to the edge of the seat as she repeatedly spasmed.

"Yeah, babe," Darius muttered, holding her in his arms as she jerked about. His erection seemed even bigger to Simone as she tried to open her eyes, but only could for a second before she was back in a physical haze of orgasm and physical ecstasy. Simone leaned forward, collapsing into his chest for a second. Lifting her, she straddled him as best she could. He turned around and sat in the seat, holding her as her legs straddled around his waist.

"How do you feel?" Darius whispered in her ear.

"You ain't right. You know it. It's wrong to do this to someone and then ask that." She chuckled.

"You feel me?"

His erection rested against her pelvic bone, between her thighs. "Hell yeah, I feel you."

Before he could say another word, she leaned back, using one arm to balance herself on his knee. With her other hand, she cupped his penis, pressing it between the folds of her love without letting him enter. She was so wet, it surprised her for a moment. Holding him firm, she slid her wet sex up and down the length of him. They both watched her rub up and down, both of them sighing. Then Darius looked past her at the overhead and groaned.

"Baby, stop. I can't take it."

Simone was just beginning. She stopped, but she slid to her knees, taking his deep erection into her mouth, her hand between her thighs. He leaned over, cupping her breast as she turned her head to the side, taking a different angle as her head slowly bobbed up and down. Suddenly, his eyes still on the screen, he jerked her head away.

"I was about to come," he explained to the questioning look in her eyes.

"I want you to come."

"No, I want to feel the inside of you first. I have to." Darius licked his lips as he spoke and then clenched his teeth. Simone slid back onto the floor.

"Babe, you got me wide open," she whispered.

"How wide?"

With her head and shoulders on the floor, she spread her legs and raised her hips, her fingers stroking in and out of her vagina. "This wide."

Darius plunged in, seeming to leap out of the seat and into her wetness in one swift move. They both shouted; Simone raised her hips, purposely trying to lock him in with each thrust. He grabbed her hips and lifted her higher into his grind, although her shoulders remained on the floor, as he bucked and jerked and released himself, both of them watching the large screen.

He collapsed on her, rolled her, and pulled him into her. "I love you," he whispered into her ear and then kissed her neck. He placed his hand on her breast and fell asleep.

CHAPTER 44

Darius was asleep. Simone did not know what made her wake up, but she was jolted from slumber. Maybe something was wrong with Jasmine. She immediately called her mother, who confirmed Jasmine was fine and asleep. Simone's throat tickled her. She wanted to get washed and be fresh and clean in case Darius woke up.

Stepping over his snoring body, Simone slowly walked out of the theatre room and stared into the picture frame. It was only then that she noticed the cluster of televisions in the wall. The security system. One screen was up, locked on Simone's car. Fascinated, Simone wondered if the system was similar to the one at work. She searched around the panel for the controls. Nothing. She remembered the large remote and tiptoed back into the theatre room, slid it from under the pile of clothes, and returned to the control room. Pressing buttons, Simone sat down at the control panel. The system was advanced but manageable. Everything was time-stamped. She wondered whether their lovemaking had been recorded. She scrolled back over the past two days. Not every encounter was recorded; in fact, most of them were not. Simone reasoned that most of his rooms were not wired for privacy. However, there she was, her legs wrapped tightly around his head, her hands grasping at the carpet, her hips gyrating until she exploded. That was yesterday when they had made love in the dining room. She never actually watched herself in the throes of passion before. Just watching Darius's intensity made her tingle, and she wanted more. She looked a damn mess, though. Hair everywhere. Her rolls were visible. She wished she had a perfect body or one that even came close. She had a bit of weight and there was no denying it on the screen. At work, the tape was like grocery store footage in a grainy black and white with faces barely recognizable. Here, the camera seemed to zoom in and out on cue, the picture was color and crisp and there she was fucking another man.

Simone shook her head but smiled. Watching Darius again made it apparent why she was hooked. What woman would not be? She fast-forwarded the tape, wondering if their early morning encounter before they both passed out and then she scrambled to work was on the tape. Nothing.

Disappointed, Simone kept scrolling through the day, looking for the last encounter. She wanted to see herself dancing just to see what she looked like. Instead, the camera came to three men sitting in the large great room. Simone zoomed past that part until something about the demeanor of one of the visitors caught her eye. If she did not know any better, she would have sworn that was…

"Jackson." His name fell from her lips and sucked all of the air out of the room. "What the hell?"

She instantly rewound the tape, unable to believe her eyes. Was this entire seduction with Darius a trap? Had Jackson arranged the entire thing so he would have proof of her infidelity and could leave her? Was Darius this cold and calculating?

She pressed play and turned up the volume.

"Babe, what are you watching?" Darius called out with his eyes closed, his face crowned from being disturbed out of his sleep.

"Nothing. Just you having a midday meeting with my husband."

Darius shot up. In seconds, he was on his feet, moving toward Simone. She jumped up with the remote in her hand.

"Did he hire you? Is that what this is, a setup?"

Darius stared at her blankly. "Simone, what are you talking about?"

"My husband is supposed to be out of town. On travel. Why else would he have been sitting in your house this afternoon, watching you sign papers? What, is Mark representing him in this? This is a way to get me out of the marriage on infidelity. You bastard! I can't believe you."

Simone backed into a corner, wanting to leave but unable to pull herself away from the tape. As the sound filled the room, Simone roared laughing. "You offered him lunch. My food, the food I cooked for you. So, what, y'all were going to watch the tape of us fucking over some nice chicken curry and vegetables?"

"Simone, think about it. That doesn't make sense. Do I need Jackson's money?"

She hesitated in mid-rant. "Then why? Why all this talk about love and future and relationship? What do you get out of siding with Jackson to set me up? Huh? I really don't mean anything to you?"

Darius took a step closer to her. "Simone, the girl that came over to the house yesterday. Tiffany. She got arrested. I cut her off because of us and she did something stupid."

"I don't give a fuck about Miss Fucking Perfect. I want to know—"

"Listen to me." Darius's voice was controlled and calm, yet strong enough to silence her. "I sent my lawyer to bail her out so I wouldn't have to see her again. Mark, that firm, is my representation."

Simone shook her head with a sly grin. "Isn't that convenient? Don't you think that's a little too coincidental?"

Darius shrugged. "Life is stranger than fiction. I didn't even know who the other guy was. I invited them in to sign the authority for them to access my funds for the bail money. Mark brought a money man with him to authorize the transaction."

"Jackson," Simone whispered.

"Jackson. I didn't say anything. I didn't mention us. That man, I don't like him, Simone. I never did."

"Why is he even in town?"

Darius shrugged, walking over to her, engulfing her in a hug. "I would never harm you. Haven't I proven that already?"

"My husband was here. I can't believe it. Maybe it's karma. Maybe it's a sign that this is wrong, that my cheating will be discovered. I mean, what are the chances?"

"I highly doubt karma is in his favor."

Simone looked at him sharply. "Of course, it is. His wife is here. Doing this. With a new baby. I'm going straight to hell." Simone chuckled bitterly, placing the remote on the sofa. She began to collect her clothing. "I have to go. Can I take a shower first?" When she turned sideways, he could see the tears spilling from her eyes.

"Simone, I wasn't going to show you this. I thought we would talk about it when the time was right." Darius rewound the tape.

"I have to go, Darius. This is so, so, so wrong and, although it feels right, I know better now. I got to make things right."

"Simone, sit down and listen. Just for a few minutes." Darius stopped the tape and fell into the sofa. "Please. Come sit down."

Simone shook her head, her face wet with guilty tears. She sat on the couch next to Darius. He kissed her on the forehead and looked deeply into her eyes. "You need to know. To open your eyes and accept the truth. This dude hasn't changed. He was like this when you were dating him and he's like it now."

"What are you talking about?"

"Just listen." Darius pressed play, his eyes never leaving Simone's face as he watched her absorb the story Jackson had shared earlier about his escapade with the lawyer.

CHAPTER 45

When he spotted the formal china on the dining room table, David sighed. There was no telling whom Celeste had invited over, or how many people he had to entertain. He walked slowly up the stairs to their bedroom and laid his jacket on the chair. Her clothes were thrown everywhere. David sat in the chair to take a breath before having to talk to Celeste. This last attack had changed things for him. It changed his perspective and his idea of their life. He could not keep living like this, giving up everything. He had to maintain some sense of home while she ran herself into the ground. Not only was it not fair, but it demonstrated her selfishness. He was simply tired of it.

A dull pain nagged at David until he snapped out of his thoughts. Standing, he lifted his jacket to find he had sat on his eyeglasses and all of her sunglasses. *Why the hell did she leave glasses in the chair?* Shaking his head, he walked slowly back downstairs.

"Hey, sweetheart," he called out. David lightened up when he glanced around the small kitchen. She wore a bikini and thong over an apron.

"Hey, yourself. I thought I would make us a meal." She laughed. "Give you something you want to eat."

David laughed aloud. "Cute." She was a lot of fun when she wanted to be. When she decided to notice him.

"Come, come on, come on." She pulled at his hands, dragging him back into the living room. The table had more decorations, finger foods, fruits, and chocolates.

"So, you're spending the evening with me tonight, huh?" He knew he sounded bitter, but he could not help it. He was somewhat past the point where wining and dining made a difference, but he loved her and would try his best. However, that part of his heart, that used to spark, no longer felt the same.

"Sit down. Let me feed you some crab dip."

Remembering the hours he spent in the bathroom after her last attempt at cooking crab dip, David shook his head with a small smile.

"What? You aren't going to eat?" Just like that, the eager smile and swinging energy had turned into anger.

"Naw, baby. I am not messing with your crab dip." David kept his voice light, his expression kind. He did not want to argue, but he was not going to be sick again.

Celeste's hand went to her hip, the serving spoon held high in the air. "Do you have any idea how much I put into making this for you? *So*, what, you aren't going to eat anything I made?"

"Why are you getting upset? I just don't want the damn dip."

"That's the problem with you. Never want to experiment or have fun. Just the same things, the same foods, the same places. Dull, dull, dull." She talked with her back to him as she walked toward the kitchen. He glared at her back, amazed at what she had said. When had the relationship become this thing? Where she would speak to him like that? He had not noticed the sarcastic tone and dismissive gestures before.

"You know," Celeste swung around on her heels, the spoon hitting the wall, "this is why I should've gone out. I tried to stay and be with you, like Simone said, but you never want excitement."

"Like Simone said?"

They stared at each other for a second, the indignant expression on Celeste's face enraging him.

"So, another woman, with a whoring husband, has to tell you to stay home with your man?"

"No." She seemed confused for a second as if she did not understand why he seemed aggravated. He studied the lines of her face, the smoothness around her eyes. She looked baby fresh, well taken care of, and healthy. He, on the other hand, had been studying the bags under his eyes that never seemed to go away. He hadn't had a decent haircut since her attack, edging up his thickened fade in the mirror with his trimmers at night.

Can I live without her? The thought swept through him and immediately guilt followed. He would never leave her, he did not think. That was why she was so spoiled. Who could deny her, hurt her, argue with her, leave her, and then face the possibility of her death or hospital visit because of the stress they caused? David suspected that sometimes she used it to her benefit, made people fall apart with guilt any time they put her in her place. He had noticed it before. How her arm or leg started hurting and she would bandage it, never saying anything, but knowing he or whoever would feel terrible. Even Simone had gone through it just a couple of weeks back. No, he would not leave. He would not argue. However, he was not going to keep living like this.

"I got some work to do."

"See what I'm talking about?" Celeste flung the wooden spoon onto the table and flopped down in the seat. All mentions of sex and flirting were over.

"Yeah, Celeste. Whatever," he barked, thinking, *She probably wasn't going to give me any, anyway.*

"Oh whatever, huh?" Celeste sat straight up, irrational anger seeming to take over again. She stuck her finger in the dip. "I'll enjoy my dip without you."

David had the urge to hurt her, to make her feel left out and alone like he had been feeling lately. He bit his tongue and walked away. Maybe she would get the hint, but most likely, she would not. Either way, he was fed up.

CHAPTER 46

J ackson sat in the dark, tapping the manila envelope Martia had given him. She did not want to give them to him, explaining the pictures seemed innocent enough, just flirtatious interaction between Simone and a man. She shouldn't even be out in public flirting, disrespecting him and their family. The more he sat in silence in the dark, the angrier he felt. *Damn her. Fucking whore. Damn her for embarrassing me and making a fool out of me. Of all people, she is fucking an NFL player. An NFL Player.* Jackson managed to forget Mark's warning and his many forgotten indiscretions.

Simone was a woman, and therefore was supposed to be at a higher level, a cleaner conscience. How did he look with a wife had by other men? He had the evidence between his fingers. Maybe he could get custody. He could have his attorney paint it like Simone left their baby so she could whore. Was that not the case this weekend, leaving Jasmine with her mother while she got her freak on?

Plus, Simone had ruined his career. There was no recovering from losing a million-dollar client unless he had another multimillion-dollar client as a replacement. This, the day after the mediation, his career at the firm was undoubtedly over.

The door finally opened; the porch light filled the hallway. *Damn bitch*, he thought. *Come on back here and get your ass busted.* Jackson relished the look of surprise, the tears, the apologies he was about to get. Finally, Simone was on the other side of this tango. She could see how humiliating this whole thing was. Unlike Simone, he was no pussy. He was not going to take her nasty ass back, no matter what she said. He respected himself more than that.

He heard her pause at the answering machine and then move slowly forward. Jackson remained at the kitchen table. When she walked in, neither spoke. Both examined each other with contempt.

"So, you made it back in town, huh?" Simone nodded at him, her eyelids were heavy, and her voice thick.

"Yep, and you finally crawled out from under your rock, huh?"

Simone watched him closely and then chuckled. "Where exactly were you while you were on travel?"

"Same place you have been all weekend. With one of my clients." Fury swept through Jackson. Simone did not seem repentant or sorry in the least bit. *Who the hell does she think she is?*

"So, you were with your client. Or you were a client? I hear sexual harassment is a hell of a charge to fight, especially for such a loyal and faithful husband as yourself." Simone's lip curled as she spoke and Jackson fidgeted nervously. She knew more than he had anticipated.

"Your weird little boyfriend filled you in, huh? Do you think he's loyal and faithful? I went to pick up his other woman for him today. Did he tell you?"

"He did. We both marveled that you managed to run and fetch her and perform your little professional duties without sticking your dick down her throat."

Jackson flinched each time Simone cursed or used a raw word. She ignored him, leaning against the wall. Jackson did not like this. How dare she say he ran and fetched anything like he was a damn servant?

"Fuck you."

"No. Fuck *you*, Jackson." She laughed a little, a bitter hateful sound. "Fuck *you* for all the bullshit I put up with! Fuck *you* from Monday to Sunday. Fuck *you* because you aren't worth it!"

"I'm not worth it? Your fat ass has some nerve." Jackson stood up, shouting at her. "I didn't sign on for this shit. Always sulking, always complaining. You had one baby and let your ass get fat. Why would I want to be with you? You don't keep yourself up and you make coming home miserable."

The smile on Simone's lips faded. He had struck a low blow, he knew, but he needed to make her hurt and take her down a little.

"Thank you, Jackson, for making this so much easier." Simone dropped her bag on the floor and studied him. "Get the fuck out!"

"Naw, this is my home. Mine and Jasmine's. Take your whoring ass to your man. You'll be crawling back when the NFL player is sleeping with a different chick a night and he gets tired of your fat ass."

"Jackson, this can be easy or hard. Either you get the fuck out, or I will call my NFL player and my baby brother. They will have no problem putting your ass out."

"You're calling that punk your man? You are a bigger fool than I thought. You are nothing to him but a fuck. Don't you get that? What part of this don't you understand? Oh, what, you're in love? Please."

Simone raised her cell phone. "I'm giving you thirty minutes to get your shit."

"Fuck that!" Jackson walked toward her in a rage. For a horrible second, he thought about hitting her but decided to brush past her. "Fuck that, this is my home! I ain't going anywhere! You're leaving. I got evidence against you. It's right here in this folder. What judge is going to put me out when I give them evidence of my wife's affair? Evidence that she left my daughter over a weekend to fuck a stranger who, by the way, is her younger brother's friend. This means at some point in the past, you must've wanted for and lusted after a child. You think between me and a lawyer, we can't take you for everything? You better leave."

Jackson heard himself rambling and screaming. He had lost control. It rarely happened, but when it did, it felt like he was outside of himself looking in. He could not stop himself. Every rational part of him was being drowned out by one emotion: hate. He hated Simone. He hated everything about her. He hated her for ruining their lives, for ruining his belief of the life they had and of what they had accomplished. He hated her having an affair, for not bowing down and apologizing as she had done so many times before. He hated her for coming home on her high horse, knowing she had been with another man, for the lack of respect and contempt she showed him. The hate overtook him.

CHAPTER 47

Simone leaned against the counter. She wanted to kill him. He had no right to talk to her that way or to treat her like that after all of his dirt.

"Didn't you just get caught fucking India's girlfriend?"

Jackson did not answer.

Simone continued. "Immediately after settling a sexual harassment hearing, at that. One that you never told me about, I might add. Let me guess, was it the same girl who called me a few months back? Yeah. How many others you think will come forward? I ain't afraid of you or your goddamn legal team. Please. You know good and well you ain't getting my daughter or my house. All you can do is scrape together what's left of your miserable existence, tuck your tail between your dog-ass legs, and leave."

Jackson spun around on his heels and squinted. "Your little affair may have cost me my job, you know."

She thought he looked like a demon and it frightened her.

"Your lover boy dropped the firm. Did you think about that, about how your shit might cost me my livelihood?"

"Please." Simone had to pretend to be unaffected. She turned her back so he could not see her face, as she walked toward the rear bathroom. "You should've thought about that before bragging about fucking around on his best friend's sister. What type of asshole does that? *You* cost us everything, not me."

At the same moment, Simone became aware that Jackson was running toward her. She felt a painful fear streak across her chest. Instinctively, she lunged forward, grabbing the knife set on the counter just as he spun her around and pinned her against the wall, his arm under her neck, her knife pressed sharply against his side.

"Don't make me stab you, Jackson. You know I will."

"How could you do this to us? You ruined everything."

"Jackson," Simone whispered, forcing air through her throat despite the pain of his arm pushing on her esophagus. "Please, don't make me do this." Tears spilled down her face, but she gritted her teeth, pressing the knife firmer against his rib cage. "Please, Jackson."

With a delirious look on his face, Jackson took a step back and Simone bent over, gasping for air. He covered his face, but his loud sobs tore through the silent house. Simone wanted to comfort him, reach out and hug him, anything to keep him from wailing. The sound felt more painful than anything she had ever heard. It was like listening to his soul tearing.

"I'm sorry, Simone," Jackson whispered through his clenched hands, tears covering his hands and face. "What did you do? What did you do?"

She did not answer him. There was nothing she could say.

"I can't lose my family. I can't lose you," Jackson continued. "Do you have any idea how you have humiliated me? Embarrassed me? Sleeping with that young boy? What the hell were you thinking? What type of sick, perverted shit is that? Were you fucking him when we were dating, when he was all of fifteen and we were twenty-one? At twenty-one, you were getting hit off by a damn child?"

"Of course not. Why are you even thinking about that? How many affairs have you had in the last three years? How many women have you run up in, making me have to use condoms every time you even think about coming near me? You're questioning me like that? Like the one time I sought attention, I caused the problem."

"You're a tramp, Simone," Jackson whispered, his hands still over his face. "The mother of my daughter is a simple tramp. I got the proof right here. I will make sure your little boyfriend sees these, too. Make sure he knows you've got more than one lover."

Simone did not know what he was talking about and she did not care. She needed to escape.

He covered his eyes again, clenching his teeth and groaning as if he were trying to keep in the pain.

Simone remained silent, tears running down her face, as she rubbed her neck. He had choked her. The husband who never laid hands on her had choked her. This no longer had anything to do with Darius or with affairs. It was about her self-preservation. Jackson was a wounded and desperate animal. He would strike the nearest and dearest to him. For the first time, she realized she could not stay with him even if she wanted to. Her marriage was over.

Simone quickly moved away from him, grabbing the manila envelope off the table.

"*Simone!* Simone…this can't happen to me. I won't let you make a fool of me…" She knew Jackson had no idea she had moved away from him. He was still facing the spot where she had stood.

With the manila envelope in hand, she picked up her bag and ran with all her strength to the front door. As the door slammed shut behind her, she heard him calling her name. She jumped into her truck and peeled out of the driveway.

Simone had no clue where to go. For the first time in her life, she was afraid. She immediately called her mother, telling her what had happened. She did not want him to get Jasmine and use the baby to lure her back to the house. She did not want him to show up at her parents' house and threaten them. She did not want to take all that drama back to Darius's house either. Eventually, she pulled into the parking lot of the mall and sat there thinking.

Opening the manila envelope, Simone gasped at the black and white photos of her at the coffee shop with Tim. The pictures seemed so intimate, although they were not touching or doing anything inappropriate. She sighed. She did not have anything else to hide. She had never been scared of Jackson before and she was not going to start now. One thing was for certain, she was not going back. Her cell phone rang.

"Where are you?" Darius's voice sounded tight. "Terence just called me, ready to leave school. Your mother is terrified and doesn't know where you are. I told him not to come home, that I would look for you."

"Why did he call you? Does he know about us?"

There was a long pause, and then Darius sighed. "He suspects. I mentioned seeing you a few times. I couldn't help it. It felt like I was betraying him if I didn't say anything at all."

"It's all right. The truth has to come out eventually. I'm at Bowie Town Center, in the parking lot in front of Macy's."

"What happened? I told you to let me follow you home."

"No, Darius, that would have just made it worse. He knew about us. He was screaming and shouting at me. Called me names—"

"Did he put his hands on you?"

"No," Simone lied. She did not want any more drama.

"Simone, did he put his hands on you?"

She did not answer.

"Listen, come here. Come stay with me."

"No, that would be wrong. My husband is losing his mind about us."

"No, he's losing his mind because he took everything he had for granted and now it's leaving him. Simone, meet me at your parents' house, all right? I just want to make sure you're safe."

Simone agreed. She hated feeling helpless and did not want to be the center of attention. However, she also felt uncertain about what the immediate future held and had no idea how far Jackson was willing to go while he blamed her.

CHAPTER 48

Jackson pulled up at her parents' house just as Simone pulled into the driveway. Simone remained in her truck with the doors locked, watching him. He got out quickly as if he did not see her, making his way to the house.

"Jackson," Simone yelled, jumping out of the truck. "Get away from my parents' house!" She ran toward the house, making a beeline for him. "Jackson, get away from my—"

He pushed her out of his way. "I'm getting my daughter, damn it! You aren't going to cost me everything. You can't just keep my daughter."

"Jackson, not like this. Don't let her see you like this."

"Get the fuck away from me, whore!" Jackson pressed the doorbell and pounded on the door while pushing Simone away.

"Jackson, these are my parents. Mine. Leave my parents' home."

"Fuck you!" Jackson pointed his finger in Simone's face as he shouted. "Get out of my goddamn way, slut!"

A black Expedition pulled into the yard just as Simone's cell phone rang. At the same time, the front door of the house flung open.

"*No,*" Simone cried out, imagining Jackson pushing past her mother and snatching her baby.

Everything seemed to move in slow motion. Simone watched Darius slide out of the huge truck as Jackson's hands pressed into her chest, slamming her against the wall of the front porch. Her head banged against the metal house number plate as Jackson yanked open the screen door. Simone slid down the wall, her head spinning.

A painful, dull, crack of flesh met flesh, sending Jackson flying through the doorframe and onto the porch. Holding her head, she watched Darius run up the steps of the porch, just missing Jackson stumbling, as he gingerly lifted her into his arms.

Mac Sheridan, someone with whom Simone never seemed to talk to anymore, who never seemed interested in her life at all, stood at the door, his arms in fighting position.

"Stand up, punk!" Simone's father danced lightly in place as if he were Muhammad Ali.

Simone did not know whether to cry or laugh. Either way, her head was aching. Darius wrapped Simone in his arms and moved off the porch.

"Are you all right?" Darius whispered.

Simone nodded. They both stared at her father.

"You gonna threaten my family? Get up, boy. I never liked your metrosexual ass, anyway."

Jackson stood up slowly, stumbling a little to the left.

"Yeah, you walked right into that left hook. Who do you think you are? Got my daughter calling us terrified for her safety, got my wife frantic that you done hurt our child. My child! My daughter! You must've lost your goddamn mind."

"No, no I just wanted—"

"Son, you better wrap up what's left of your pride and get your ass outta here! Now I done watched what you put my child through. I don't say much, I figure she's a woman so I'll leave it up to her mother. Don't take my silence for not loving my daughter. Don't think we ain't got her back. You hear me?" Mac stepped closer to Jackson. "This is my baby and my grandbaby. I will take you outta this world, even if I got to spend the rest of my days behind bars, before I let you put fear in them."

Jackson stared at the short, stout light brown man in front of him. Simone's father was an ex-cop. It occurred to Simone that Jackson was slowly remembering that and the fact that Mac Sheridan kept several guns locked up in the cabinet in the garage. He glanced at Simone quickly as if seeing her for the first time. Purposely ignoring Darius, Jackson sighed, turned on his heels and walked back to his car, shaking his head.

"Simone, you okay, baby? I don't know what that fool was thinking, but don't worry, baby. You got me and your mom. You hear me?" He hesitated, staring at the man holding her. "D. Winfield? What you doing here, boy? Damn, look at you, son, you done got huge. Margarite, come look who's here."

Simone stood still for a minute, allowing the feeling of parental love to invade her mind and heart. In the moment of chaos, the man who meant the most had protected her, despite her wrongs, her faults, and her flaws. Her daddy had vocalized his unconditional love for her and her child, and she never realized how much she needed to hear it until that moment. It had not occurred to her how much she needed her father to reaffirm her.

Wrapped in Darius's arms and emotionally wrapped in her father's heart, Simone stepped into her parents' house, feeling like a renewed woman, like someone was finally loving Simone.

About the Author

JESSICA TILLES is an award-winning, national bestselling author of several books, and the 2008 African American Literary Awards Show "Independent Publisher of the Year" award recipient. She has ghostwritten many books through the Literary Ghostwriter and is the owner of TWA Solutions & Services (formerly The Writer's Assistant), a service dedicated to helping authors accomplish their dreams of publishing their books, as well as providing other literary services. She resides in Maryland with her four fury babies: Chelsea, Chanel, Piccachu, and Cinnamon.

Visit Jessica Tilles online at:
www.jessicatilles.com
www.twasolutions.com
www.literaryghostwriter.com
www.xpressyourselfpublishing.com

Follow Jessica Tilles on Social Media:
Twitter, Instagram, LinkedIn: @JessicaTilles
Facebook: @JessicaTillesAuthor